Black Rain

To Eric,

much *Respect*.

you be cool.

Black Rain

Published by We Must X-L Publishing
Kansas City, Missouri

Printed in the United States of America
Cover by Lydell Jackson/Ulisa Lathon
Photography by Gerald Grimes

ISBN 0-9749564-0-6

PUBLISHER'S NOTE
This is a work of fiction. Names, characters, places, and incidents are either the product of
the author's imagination or are used fictitiously, and any resemblance to actual persons, living
or dead, business establishments, events, or locales is entirely coincidental.

Black Rain

Vincent R. Alexandria

special thanks

I have to give thanks to God Almighty for his works and blessings He has bestowed upon and within me. To my children; Randi, Preston, Royce, Azia, and Nia, you are the poetry and creativity within me and without your joy and laughter my life would not mean anything. I love you with all that I am.

To my parents and family, for all the love, support, laughter, and prayers that you all have shared for me, thank you. You have made my life rich and full of love.

For my best friend's in the world, Derrick, Gino, and John, you guys have had my back from the beginning and keep me spiritually grounded. Thanks for the 25 years of love and brotherhood.

I can't say enough to my ace-in-the-hole, Victor McGlothin, your friendship in undeniable and I would die for you my brother. Keep practicing on them bones and I'll let you win one day. (Smile) To my editor, Susan Malone, you bring out the best in me.

Thanks to all the great authors that have supported the Brother 2 Brother Literary Symposium. We are making a difference promoting reading and literacy in America, thanks for believing in the vision.

acknowledgements

They say a person is as good as the people that supports him and I want to thank all those who have supported me in my writing endeavors; Jeanette Lewis, Patricia Oliver, The Rev. & Mrs. Gary Jones, Mother Jones, Jimmy "Jet" Alexander, Bernice McFadden, M.C. Richardson, Women of Wisdom Book Club - San Antonio, St. Louis Church Family,& Fr. John, Marie Young, Frederick & Venetta Williams, Linda Martin, Candice, Travis Hunter, Jackson Mississippi Book Club, Zane, Women of Word Book Club, Lorrie Goings, Eric Pete, Linda Alexandria, Katie Wine, Aaron Johnson, Jr. II, Perry Alexandria, Donald Johnson, Frederick Williams, Lorrie Goings, William Cooper, Tracey Grant, Regina & Beverly, Emma Rodgers, Mosaic Books, Cynthia Guidry, Cheryl Shelvin, Kimberla Lawson Roby, John and Karen Ashford, Sr., C. Kelly Robinson, Parry Brown, Sara Freeman Smith, Nina Foxx, Jacquese Silvas, Brenda Thomas, Evelyn Palfrey, Blair Walker, Dionne Driver, Sean Tyler, 103.3 FM-KPRS and the Carter Broadcast family, Greg Love, Lady T, Tre' Michaels and 107.3 FM Radio Station, The KC Negro Baseball Museum-Bob Kendrick and Johnnie Lee, Arzelia Gates and the Gates family, Victoria Christopher Murray, Donald, Lillian, & Albert Dean (Cuz), Mom & Dad Ashford, Alvin Brooks, Mom & Granny Young, Uncle Pete, Bob O'Brian, Damon Smith, Elaine Dibartilo, Frances Latimer, Gerald Grimes-the greatest photographer in the world, Ulisa Latham, Sheila Goss, Sheila Shelvin, Ilyasah Shabazz, Delores Thornton, Michelle Chester, Nichole Poignord, Jamila

Jagours, Katie Gibson, Kwame Alexander, Steve Perry, Lisa Cross, Lydell Jackson-the best artist in the world, Rosemary Kelly, Monica Miller, Dino Anderson, Omar Tyree, Patricia Haley, Peggy Hicks - the most spectacular friend and publicist in the world, Philena Wesley, PJ Jones, Quiana Williams, Renetta Davis, Cousins Verneal, Marilyn, Thelma, and Denita, Mary Jones, Pam & Rufus Williams, Steven Barnes, and to any others I forgot, I'm sorry! (Smile)

prologue

THE RINGING PHONE AT THE HOME OF DETECTIVE JOE Johnson screams through the dark silence. No one is home. On the fourth ring call notes activates.

A woman speaks on the end of the receiver in a panicked tone, just over a whisper. "Joe, this is Chase. I'm in too deep. I need your help. Please!"

The red light from the caller ID illuminates in the darkness, flashing with urgency every few seconds like a distress signal from a ship that is sinking.

one

.

STARS RADIATE AGAINST THE BLACK SEPTEMBER NIGHT
sky and the full moon glows benignly. As the crisp night air flows through
the crack in my window, I look at my family asleep in the van and am grateful for the life with which God has blessed me.

I am Joe Johnson, Chief Detective of the Kansas City, Missouri
Homicide Unit, but tonight I am a husband and father returning home
from an evening of fun with my family. Kansas City, a growing mid-west
metropolis is known for great jazz and barbecue. This city of fountains is
a great place to live and work.

My partner Vernon Brown and I have received two promotions in the
last two years, and my former Captain has made Commissioner. We
recently elected a Black Mayor, and our city government is probably as
diverse and progressive for African Americans as any in the United States.

The Commissioner, Vernon, and I all moved up the ranks together.
We've all earned it. Our department has one of the highest solved-case
files in the Midwest Region, which allows me to spend more time with my
family, and I take advantage of all the time I can.

The soft light of the moon caresses the lovely features of my wife
Sierra. The mellow beams dance across her deep cleavage and I can't wait

to put the kids to bed and let the romance of the full moon capture Sierra and me seductively in its grip.

Our two-year-old twins, Vernie, named after my partner and best friend, Vernon Brown, and my namesake, Joe Jr., are strapped in their child seats. Their heads slump forward, each hand gripping circus balloons. We were blessed to have a girl and a boy as twins.

Nia, now four years old and as beautiful as ever, sits between them. Her pink and blue cotton candy, secure in her plastic bag, lies on her lap, with remnants of the sugary treat coating her cherubic face. I smile and breathe a heavy sigh as I turn onto our block and pull into the driveway.

We had such fun at the Univer-Soul Circus, the only African-American circus of its kind on tour. We laughed, cheered, and were awed by the magnificent show full of great acts and African history told by the Ringmaster. His sidekick, Zeke the midget, stole the show with his humor, antics, and dancing. We felt as if we were part of the act with the participation and great music. Life doesn't get any better than this.

After putting the children to bed and taking my shower, I slip into my pajama pants and walk over to the bed where Sierra lies, wearing one of my oversized Rockhurst College T-shirts.

She is, however, fast asleep. I smile, give way to my erection, brush her hair to the side, and kiss her softly on the forehead. I promise to wake up early before the kids to say good morning to my wife, the Big Daddy way. In an attempt to calm the disappointment of romance on hold, I go downstairs and into the kitchen to satisfy my other weakness.

I put a couple of scoops of Neapolitan ice cream into a cup, head into the living room compromising, happy, and humming the words, "I scream, you scream, we all scream for ice cream." Then I put the receiver to my ear to check our messages.

My heart flutters and my gut tightens at the anxiety and fear in FBI Agent Chase's voice. She has to be in desperate trouble to call me at home. She graduated at the top of her class at the FBI Training Academy, and is more than capable of handling herself with a prodigious IQ, common sense, and a black belt in karate.

I knew she was going undercover, but she did not inform me about the particulars of this case. Chase is a friend of the family. We've worked together on a serial-killer assignment, and a couple of drug cases that ended up on my desk because they were homicides. We'd been somewhat intimate, but had not gotten personal after that. She respected my feelings for my family, and knew I would never leave my wife.

Chase also saved my life when we were working on the assignment of two escaped convicts. Deep in the mountains on a manhunt, I came across one of the escaped killers getting water from a spring. As I confronted the convict and apprehended him, a shot rang out. Chase shot the other escapee, who had been silently sneaking up behind me with an ax held over his shoulder.

I put down the ice-cream-filled spoon from my mouth and immediately dial the number of the one person who can explain the project Chase is working. A queasiness of fear builds in my gut. I don't like what I am feeling; fearing the unknown; that circumstances are about to be out of my control. The chance that dues are about to be paid...

"Hello!" Agent Royal James answers gruffly, awakened from a deep sleep. We've worked on several cases together, and Vernon and I have even done cooperative work with the Federal Bureau of Investigations. Agent James is a lead Officer in Charge, which is the equivalent of Captain of a Police Department.

"Royal, Johnson here. I got a message from Chase. She says she's in need of help and is working deep undercover. I need to know what case she's working, the circumstances of the mission, and the players involved. I fear for her life. I've never known her to sound the way she did. She sounded desperate."

After a long silence, Agent James blurts, "Joe, we can't talk over the phone. Let's meet in thirty minutes at the place where we had lunch the last time we were together." James hangs up leaving me no choice but to meet him. I hate it when people do that.

The last place we had lunch was at the Longview Lake Marina. We like Jeffrey Bradley, the hotdog vendor. He doubles as a snitch and gives us great information as well as discounts on the food. We caught Jeffrey several times trying to pickpocket people on the pier.

He once even tried to pickpocket Vernon, which was the last straw. After Vernon slapped him around a bit, he decided to work for us. We pay him pretty well. Longview Lake is about twenty minutes from my home. I frequent the lake, riding fifteen miles a day on the park bike trail.

I go upstairs and throw on some jeans, sneakers, and an old Baker University T-shirt I bought after Graduate School, and leave a note on the nightstand for Sierra in case she wakes. She can reach me on my cell phone anytime. I grab my ankle holster and .25 automatic pistol, take the keys to my black 300 Nissan convertible, and head for Longview Lake.

The marina is isolated. I sit in the car listening to the autumn leaves rustling in the night wind. The night sky is majestic in its crisp, starlit display.

The fishy smell of the lake water, the view of the wooded area, and the rhythmic sound of the waves splashing against the rocks have a way of putting one in a state of meditation. One of the reasons I enjoy biking in this area is the array of beautiful colors now in the autumn leaves.

Time melts like the ice cream in my cup at home. Agent James eventually pulls up in his new, navy blue 944 Porsche. We get out and exchange greetings. James is a stout, bald man. Taller than me at six feet, two inches, weighing about 190 pounds, with brown skin, he appears neat and pristine like a Federal Agent about to go into the office; even his hooded sweat suit has ironed creases in it.

We walk over to the dew-covered boat dock and have a seat on a bench facing the lake. Agent James's dark eyes dart back and fourth as if he expects something to jump out at us. He frowns as he wipes the sweat from his brow. I've never seen him look like this before.

"Joe what I'm about to tell you is top-secret shit and once I tell you, you're involved. So, if you really don't want to get into this, walk away now."

Agent James struggles with his shaking hands to light a cigarette. We stare at each other for a minute. My first thought is to walk away. Life is good and I really don't need any problems, but the loyalty to Chase leaps up.

"I've never known you to smoke, Royal."

He takes a long drag from the cancer stick and exhales a big cloud of smoke.

"I haven't smoked since college. I've always kept it together, but this case that Chase is on is one of the biggest cases I've ever handled in the Mid-West Region, and I don't know how high up this thing goes. It's a great possibility my phone is tapped and I've been followed on several occasions. Agent Purvis Smelley is missing as well and could be as good as dead. We have a burned body at the morgue that matches his body dimensions. We're waiting on dental records."

Agent James lets out a long belch and holds his stomach. "I hate burn victims because it can take so much time to identify them. It can set a case back weeks. Neither Chase, nor Smelley has reported in for the last six weeks. They were on this assignment together. So, you in or out?"

He flicks the half-smoked cigarette into the waves of the lake and looks me squarely in the eyes. The current takes hold of the butt and carries it further away. I feel as though I'm about to be carried away from all that I care for and hold valuable. But I can't bear the thought of someone harming Chase.

What will Sierra say? Am I truly doing this for the right reason? I can't forget my partner, Vernon. His reaction to me going on this case alone will be just short of a heart attack. Without hesitation Chase would risk her life for me; shit, she already has.

"I'm in!"

Agent James pulls a folder and bulky envelope from his trousers that has been hidden behind his pullover sweatshirt. "Joe, several officers and agents have come up dead. I'm sure you've heard of the car fires lately?"

I nodded. "The reporters seem to think that they're gang related. Some kind of retaliation for gang-bangers disrespecting each others' turf."

With a half-smile Agent James opens the folder. "That's the bullshit we've been feeding the press. The media loves gang hype. They bite every time we fish that story to them. 'Ghetto Paranoia' sells! The truth of the matter is, every one of the victims has been in law enforcement. They have been professional hits."

James moves the folder into the rays of the overhead lamppost that lights the dock and pulls out photos of bodies burned so badly that they were unrecognizable.

In some instances the gold chains, clothes, and jewelry are burned into the flesh, making them look as one. One picture is a montage of black, brown, and red burned flesh. The heat was so intense that it burned deep enough to expose bone matter.

"Joe, the stuff doesn't stop here; we have the exact same situation going on in Nebraska, Kansas, Oklahoma, and Iowa. We feel they're all connected. In these states, there is Federal law injunctions on state and local law-enforcement agencies and their handling of drug money seized from drug busts. This leads to illegal search and seizures where officers are hitting up known drug suspects when it is believed they have large amounts of cash on hand. These large amounts of money can't be traced, and the drug lords can't report the stolen money to the police. So we have two things that can happen: they buy the police or start a war with them. That can't happen, Joe."

'To protect and collect' is the motto people are using on the street for police these days," I say.

Agent James sighs heavily. "We don't know how many dirty cops are on the take, but we do know that once you're in this black ring, death is the only way out. We have reason to believe that these hits are internal. A 'black rain,' if you will. Dirty cops, killing other dirty cops. Agents Chase and Smelley infiltrated the ring in Nebraska. Last I heard she'd got next to the leader of these rogue cops, a guy they call Dread. That's him on the fourth photo. He's one bad dude Joe. A former Marine. You can see by the size of him that he can be an intimidator."

Dread is Cuban looking. His real name is Orlando Cattanno. He's a muscular guy with a tattoo on his forearm of the Harley-Davidson emblem.

"Shit, looks like I'm going to have to brush up on my motorcycle riding and hit the gym a little harder, just in case I have to match up to this guy," I think aloud.

I keep flipping through the pictures and see this huge white man who looks to be Cattanno's right-hand man. Underneath his picture is the name, Rick "Brutus" Tucker. I sit back abruptly as the next picture reveals Agent Chase holding Cattanno's arm as the big guy, Brutus, opens the back of the black Lincoln Continental for them.

Chase is beautiful as ever with her caramel skin. She wears dark shades and her silky, black hair is much longer than I've ever seen it. Her leather pantsuit reveals the body that my fingertips explored the night we spent in Jefferson City after questioning Missouri's Governor. What are you into Chase?

"I'm going to need a couple of days to get things straight with my partner and family," I explain.

"Joe, This group operates out of Nebraska, they like to move around a lot. He always keeps five or six guys around him. Chase is using her real name on this one, because her background is better than one we could make up. She was a cop before making the Bureau. This Dread fella likes a smart woman. The only thing he doesn't know about Chase is that she's FBI. I'll clear it with Commissioner Wayne, but no one else must know. You understand you're flying blind on this one. You have my pager number. Use a pay phone and make sure you use it in transit. Don't use a phone close to where you'll be staying, because I'm sure they'll be monitoring you, so you have to remain evasive. I'll make some inside contacts for you in each state."

Agent James lights another cigarette, breathes the smoke in deeply, and exhales. "The agents will contact you when you let me know where you are. Good luck, Johnson. You can pick a car up at the FBI compound, and I'll make sure it's loaded with weapons in a secret compartment in the trunk. Everything else you need, will be in the envelope I gave you."

We shake hands and he walks back to his car and drives off into the night. I take a deep breath of the damp night air and sit under the lamp-post while going over the other material fingering through surveillance pictures of Chase, the guy they call Dread, and a few other cronies. Chase has dyed her hair a sandy brown. It hits her just below her shoulders. It looks nice on her.

I open the envelope and there is what looks to be about fifty thousand-dollar bills. Agent James has always had a sense of humor. Is that what my life is worth these days? I place the money back in the envelope and tuck it into my trousers. The last thing I need is to get hit up before getting a chance to use it. Life is full of surprises, and death has a funny way of making you see what's important real quick. Right now, reality is staring me square in the face and I wonder can I fit that bill?

two

CHASE LETS THE WHITE PLUSH COTTON ROBE SLIDE FROM her body, and it seems funny, even cynical, that her name is embroidered on the lapel of the robe. Chase never noticed that when she opened the yellow ribbon-adorned, white box. This is the first time she has worn this newly delivered gift from Dread. In the shower, she slowly turns the levers, letting the steam and water consume her.

She tries, to no avail, to fight back the tears of fear as the goose bumps that have collapsed upon her skin give voice to her tormented emotions. She strives to grab her inner strength to battle the abandonment and loneliness. She struggles desperately to remember the teachings of her former karate Sensei, and the power of focused and disciplined meditation.

"An arrow that is shot without aim is a useless weapon. Know the source of your target and shoot strong and straight, so that the arrow may go through it and not simply pierce it. A small wooden arrow can stop a full grown bear, if your aim is focused and true." She smiles at the words of the small biscuit-brown man with a head full of graying hair and a neatly trimmed goatee.

He looked frail, but was graceful in his motions and could withstand the attack of five grown men. Sensei Gadson taught her inner peace and discipline. For that she is so grateful, especially now when her very existence is on the verge of being shattered.

The hot water streams down her and she thinks of the one thing that always gives her a sense of safety and security, Detective Joe Johnson. She envies his wife so much. If Chase could take her place for one day and have him all to herself, she would know true happiness.

Thoughts of Joe, brings her a small smile; it is only a matter of time before he comes to help her out of this deadly situation. Chase has always been secure in knowing that she can take care of herself. But to get out of this situation, she'll need help. She's yet to come up against a psychopath like Orlando "Dread" Cattanno.

Chase can't stand the sight or smell of him, nor the thought of herself being undercover as his woman. She's in deadly deep. If her cover is blown, she's as good as dead. Chase hasn't heard from Agent Smelley in a week, and Dread has doubts about him and his loyalty to the organization. God, let him be careful and safe. If not for the thought of imagining Joe every time Dread touches her, her cover would have been blown a long time ago.

She slowly starts to enjoy the water pulsating against her skin. The agent imagines Joe as the water streams from her face, down her neck, and flows over her breasts and nipples. The hot water streams down her arms, over her belly button, cascading between her legs, and toes. She slowly caresses her shoulders, hugging herself.

The million droplets of water are like tiny fingers affectionately caressing her skin. Her ecstasy rises as she imagines Joe entering her. She pulls her sandy-brown, shoulder-length hair out of her face and begins to stroke her clitoris until her body trembles uncontrollably, and she falls breathless against the white tile wall. Weak at the knees, she holds onto the soap dish for balance and giggles at the thought of Detective Joe Johnson seeing her this way.

Chase smiles, soaps her sponge, and washes away the pleasure she has called forth. As she rinses off, the shower door is yanked open. She pulls the shaving razor from its place, flips it open, and holds it at the culprit's throat.

"Ohhhh, baby, you kno' I love it when you play rrroouugh," Dread says as he eases his neck away from the sharp blade and hands her a towel. "Hurry up, you makes me late for my appointmunt, yes?" He commands with his thick Cuban accent. His breath smells of a freshly smoked Cuban cigar. He stands there as she covers herself from his gaze and folds the razor, putting it back into its place. He smiles as he checks his throat for blood in the mirror. He is handsome with slick, jet-black hair, a neatly trimmed thin mustache, and a body like Mike Tyson's. His deep reddish-brown skin is flawless, except for the cut on his right cheek he received from a fall as a child riding his bike.

Dread slaps her rear as Chase walks by. She turns and rolls her eyes mischievously. "I should slit your throat and kill you for doing that shit."

She grabs a pair of jeans, a pull-over top, and a pair of matching slip-on pumps, and carries them to the bed. She applies Bath-Sheba shea butter to her body, combs her hair, and puts on her clothes.

"I love it when you wear nothin' under your clothes. It tis' so sexy, eh?" Dread embraces her from the back and slowly grinds while kissing her neck.

His thick erection pokes her and she swallows the bile that has risen in her throat from disgust. She plays it cool and pulls herself free.

"Remember, we're late, Cattanno. I need to make up my face," she reminds him.

"Dat's right, we are, and you'll have to remind me to make up for rushing you, my dear. I'll be waiting in the auto-mo-bile," Dread says as he slaps her rear again.

The tension ties up in her shoulders and she wants to pick up something and bust him in the back of the head. That would be a death wish with at least six armed and loyal bodyguards at the house at all times, so she sits and applies makeup as angry tears fills her eyes.

"Please hurry up, Joe, and get me out of this shit."

She walks down the solid oak staircase from the second-floor bedrooms, reaches under her shirt and removes her small .25 caliber handgun and takes it off safety. As she gets to the foyer, two Nebraska cops appear to escort her. The first is Ronnell Jenkins, a stubby black guy from Louisiana with blue-black skin, bright ivory teeth, and very pink gums. It almost makes him look like a Deep South cartoon stereotype.

The other cop, Stanley Turner is called 'Weasel' because of his long nose and beady eyes set so close together. They double as Dread's bodyguards. Chase is led through the game room that holds a big-screen TV, ping-pong table, pool table; several arcade games, and an eight-seat mini-theater.

They enter a large hallway with a white Roman imported marble floor. Several expensive vases and pillars hold busts of Roman Emperors. They sit proudly as if condoning her present plight. They proceed to the side entrance where the luxury fleet of cars sits near the estate drive and garage.

The head security guard, Brutus Tucker, greets us. "I'll take it from here, fellas."

Brutus relocated from Portland, Oregon after tiring of the rampant gang problems. Kids were killing kids for senseless reasons. He transferred to the Nebraska Police Department five years ago and hooked up with Dread. Brutus' square chin reminds her of Dudley DooRight on steroids. He often gets in trouble for letting his blonde hair creep just below regulation of the department's grooming policy.

He loves classic Harley-Davidson motorcycles and happens to be a "crack mechanic," thus, Dread's interest of a fellow biker with skills unmatched by any bike mechanic in Nebraska. At six feet-eight inches tall with a boyish grin, he has a tendency to be flirtatious with the ladies, including Chase when Dread isn't around. They often pass the time playing cards. They both love spades and play pity-pat for a quarter a game.

Brutus gives the other crony guards a nod and they obediently climb into a black Suburban SUV.

"Hello, Ms. Chase."

"Hello, Brutus, and how are you this Friday evening?" Brutus has always been respectful and nice to her. Not like the other 'yes men' that cower at Dread's very words.

"I'm doing fine, just fine. You be careful tonight," he beckons with dark troubled eyes as though he wants to warn me of something but can't.

Chase inches into the back seat and tries to fight her urge to run. Something is about to go down. Something is terribly wrong and Dread wears this smirk like a revelation is coming. He slides next to her and puts his arm around her neck.

"You kno' loyalty is very much important to me. Why, I jus' don't know what I would do wit' myself if something abouts you is untrue. I would just go crazy and someone would have to die, of course," he says, looking her in the eyes.

She puts her hand close to her gun and contemplates killing him right there. Just surviving jumping from the car could have fatal consequences, so she plays it cool.

"And give up all this? Don't be silly, Dread. You spoil me and take care of me. What else could a woman ask for?"

He kisses her on the forehead and sits back reclines in his seat with his hand on her thigh, saying nothing the rest of the ride.

They ride into the sprawling suburbs of Nebraska and turn onto a deserted dirt country road near Freemont, just off Highway 30. About a half a mile up the road is a silo and big red barn with a Nebraska corn-husker emblem painted on one side. A big smiley-faced blonde red-neck with straw hanging out of his mouth dressed in black overalls adorned by a big red Nebraska 'N' stands on the front.

The Cartoon Character also has on a white shirt with an ear of corn hanging out of his front pocket, a big red hat on his head, and holds a football in his right arm. A couple of Nebraska police vehicles sit parked by the barn and the field next to it has about fifty head of cattle mulling around.

Ronnell shouts out like an old house Negro, "We're here, boss!"

"Berry good, let's get dis over wit," Dread says while rubbing his hands together.

Chase frowns, "What is this, Dread? Why are we out in the middle of nowhere at some stinking barn? Why did you drag me out here? I'm not impressed, honey." She stays in her seat in protest.

She feels that if she enters that barn her life is going to end or change drastically. There is nothing in the area for miles, just dirt and straw. The setting sun colors the rusted sky with blue, orange, red, and yellow. A water trough overflows next to a big chunk of licking salt. The rest of the area is miles of plowed fields, naked of its harvest.

"Dis is a time of reckoning, baby. The truff will set you free and shit like dat dare," Dread says, laughing as he enters the barn. "Get her, gentlemun, and bring her wit' us," Dread commands.

"Take your fucking hands off me. Let me go, you bastards!" Chase screams as she punches and kicks at Weasel and Ronnell as they enter the SUV from both sides and grab her feet and arms.

"Let her go, fellas. Chase, calm down and c'mon," Brutus orders as he places his hand on his .44 Magnum. He gives her a smile and a wink. But she know he'll use it, if he has to.

The two goons let Chase go and she straightens her clothes and follows them into the huge aged barn with Brutus bringing up the rear. This brings being scared to a new level.

The musty, dusty, and dark barn smells like husked corn. At the rear lanterns glow with something that's hanging from the beam that parallels the vaulted ceiling. Faint moans sound of someone in pain, and as she gets closer, that someone slowly comes into view.

Everything within her flows up to her throat. Panic slithers up Chases's spine as goose-bumps invade her skin. The thought of being exposed as a FBI Agent is at the forefront of Chase's mind as her partner and fellow agent, Purvis Smelley, dangles from a rope. His wrists are bleeding from the thick, coarse rope. Blood flows from a laceration across his left brow and lower lip. The blood has made a trail down the front of his shirt and pants leg and slowly drips from the tip of his shoes and forms a figure eight of congealed blood as he at a snail's pace swings from the rope, back and forth.

Smelley gradually looks up as if he can feel her presence. He blinks away the blood that is dripping into his eyes. He smiles at her then lowers his head. Three of his front teeth are missing from his blood-covered mouth. She prays to God to <u>please</u> don't let him blow her cover.

She wonders how she will get out. How will she get Smelley out before he gets killed? Her gun has six bullets and eight men stand around Smelley, not counting the four that are with them. Even if she gets Agent Smelley down, he'll be in no shape to help her take on this motley crew. If only Joe were here.

Dread saunters around Smelley, sizing him up.

"Weeelll, it does do look like he knows you berry well, my darling." Dread looks at Smelley and Chase for a reaction.

She swallows hard and tries to control her breathing. "Don't be ridiculous. You need to let that poor man loose. You've made your point. He's in enough pain, Dread." Unfortunately with the dire situation, that's all she could come up with.

Dread smiles as he stares at the both of them. His motley crew moves in closer, weapons drawn, anticipating a show down, revelation, or an end to this situation. All is quiet, except the sound of the coughing up of blood that Smelley is making as he dangles from the rope, sweating and bleeding at the same time.

Dread pulls out a switchblade and walks up to Chase and places it at her throat. As she tries to move his arm, two of his men grab her.

"This shit ain't funny, Dread."

"No, it 'tis not. But you need to tell me the truff. Are you the FBI? You know dis' man? You been plotting against me like dis' fucking cock-a-roach? Are you trying to destroy everything that I have built? I was smart enough to have the phone tapped and dat's how I caught this son-of-a-pig reporting me to the FBI. I always knew it was something about that guy I did not like, but you, Chase, hmmm. I love you and it's killing me to think dat' you could be party to my demise wit' dis' piece of shit."

Dread's face is touching hers. The spittle from his speech sprinkles her cheek. He has a fist full of her hair and has her head pulled back so her throat is exposed to the sharp edge of the blade.

"Just like I thought!" Smelly begins. Dread, you aren't anything but a little punk picking on women. I don't know that lady. This shit is between you and me, asshole. I came in alone, but others will follow and take your punk ass down. Now come over here and lick my balls, you Cuban bitch!" Smelley laughs.

Dread looks around at the others in the room and becomes enraged. His complexion turns red as his body trembles and his lip quivers at the disrespect. He releases Chase's hair and runs his fingers through his own. His eyes roll back into his head as his face distorts with anger. "Lick your balls? You tell me to lick your balls in front of my woman? Oh yes, my friend, you are one crazy cock-a-roach."

Dread charges over and stabs him in the stomach and chest repeatedly as Smelley jerks from the force of the blows. Blood spills from his body and mouth. The rope jerks and swings.

Smelley's body becomes limp. The kicking and jerking stops. His bladder and bowels release and forms a puddle of fowl stench at his feet. Dread wipes his knife off on Smelley's shirt and spits toward the ground at the urine and defecation now being absorbed by the straw and dirt floor. Then he pushes the bloodied and soiled body away from him.

He walks up to Chase, places his blood-drenched hand to her face, cupping it, and pushing the tip of his switchblade toward her right eye. The tip of the blade touches her eyelash. He brings his face so close to hers, she can feel his breath.

"If I even thought you were a Fed, I'd cut both your eyes out and gut you like a pig." Dread looks for a reaction from her and she gives none. He smiles and kisses her. "Let's get out of here!"

The men release her and walk away. Chase pulls her gun and fires two shots over their head. They turn with guns drawn, and she aims at the rope suspending Agent Smelley. She fires one shot and the rope comes free as Smelley's body collapses on the ground.

Tears of rage flow from her face as if she doesn't care if she dies at this point. They have killed her friend and she has been disrespected. She goes against everything her Karate instructor had taught her. She let her anger control her actions. Shit, she wants revenge and she wants to fight.

"If you fuckers ever put your hands on me again, I will kill each one of you and your mothers that gave birth to you."

Dread laughs, "Ooh, you know I like it when you talk dirty to me. Bring her along."

She put her gun away as Weasel and Ronnell comes toward her. She takes a stance and braces herself for battle. They look at the other men, then to Dread.

Weasel throws up his hands in confusion, "What's this? You gotta be fuckin' kiddin' me, lady. Come on before we have to hurt—"

She does a flying drop kick to Weasel's face and knocks him over one of the cattle stalls. Dust rises from where he lands. She faces Ronnell, ready. Anger boils inside of her and Chase wants to hurt somebody the way Smelley was killed. She refuses to cry or show weakness and knows this will play into her survival.

All the attention is on her. The men encircle the defiant woman. Dread stands with his beefy arms folded, grinning devilishly at what is unfolding. He waves his hand and two more men attack. The female under-cover agent drops to the ground and swing-kicks the first, bringing him to the ground. She crushes her elbow into his throat. She gets back to her feet and kicks the other in the groin. He reaches down to grab his genitals. Chase brings her knee up to his forehead with swift force, knocking him backward and unconscious.

Another attacker grabs her left shoulder. She slams an elbow to his nose. It breaks on contact. She pivots and thrusts her palm upward into the nasal cavity of the assailant to her right. An upward thrust-kick to the face sends the attacker spinning to the ground in pain.

Dread grows tired of the fight. "Brutus, end this!"

Brutus comes to face the embattled woman. She sizes up the mammoth man, all of six feet-eight inches and easily 320 pounds. She wipes the sweat from her brow and takes her stance. Brutus is one big son-of-a-bitch, but Chase has a 'fuck 'em all' attitude.

Brutus pleads, "Don't make me do this, Chase."

She looks at Brutus. "Whatever!" She says, steadying herself for his attack.

Dread looks at his watch and snarls, "Get to it, Man!"

She runs and jumps into a flying drop-kick. Brutus grabs her in mid-air and slams her into the dirt floor. Dirt, dust, and straw fly around her like an explosion. All of the electricity in her body leaches into the floor as the wind escapes her lungs.

Dirt and blood fill her mouth. She is picked up off the floor. Brutus has her by the throat with one hand. Chase struggles, but the pain is too great. Unable to grasp air into her lungs, she starts to black out.

The last thing she hears is, "Throw the bitch in the car!"

three

UP EARLY SATURDAY MORNING AFTER HAVING A RESTLESS NIGHT, I have just finished walking five miles on the treadmill and lifting weights for forty minutes. Putting on my boxing gloves, I take to the punching bag. It's always relaxing, exercising to the oldies station Magic 107.3 and Lady T playing groups like the GAP Band, LTD, James Brown, BT Express, Roberta Flack, Donnie Hathaway, Midnight Starr, The Time, Prince, Klymax, and George Clinton.

The girl is just jammin' commercial-free, and my hands keep rhythm with the drum's beat as I attack the suspended heavy bag. I bob and weave to the melodic sounds doing a dance step with the bag, adding in an additional cabbage-patch move as I groove to "For Those Who Like To Groove," by the group Raydio featuring Ray Parker, Jr.

I am instantly mesmerized by the sweet/salty smell of bacon and eggs descending from the kitchen. Sierra's Saturday breakfast is always a treat. I stop working out long enough to take a deep breath of fresh dough biscuits and imagine Sierra buttering the golden brown tops the way the kids and I like them.

The laughter of mischievous children fills the air. My impish crew is trying to be in stealth mode. I pretend to be in full concentration and commence with my workout. The kids don't think I see them in their Animaniac cartoon character pajamas, sneaking up on me from the back stairwell. Nia, who is four, as pretty as an angel with a head full of pig tails and quite the intelligent one for her age, leads the playful assailant two-year-old twins. Vernie, with that dimple-filled smile, can melt me into her wishes with the bat of her hazel eyes. She is just as beautiful as her mother. Joe Jr., who has his thumb in his mouth, looks more like me every day. I really can't remember being that bad, though. That kid gets into everything, and Curious should be his middle name. They are hilarious as they follow close behind Nia, giggling the whole time. I bite my lower lip to keep from laughing.

I continue to bounce and pounce on the beanbag, making sure my back's to them, but watch their shadows cast by the morning sunlight. As soon as they get close enough to the mat, I turn and grab them all in one big tackle, laughing with them as they scream in sweaty surprise.

Nia yells, "Ugh, Daddy, you're sweaty and stinky!

Let us go!" All the kids scream in unison laughing the whole time.

I say in my best Darth Vader voice, "Naw, I got y'all now and you will pay for coming into the lair of the stinky monster."

We all wrestle on the floor and I see Sierra's slippers descending the stairwell with an edge of determination. She proceeds toward us, and even the kids can sense that we are in trouble as she stands in her green sweat pants, a Bernice McFadden T-shirt of the novel, <u>Sugar</u>, and her robe open as she has her hands on her hips.

"Okay, children, get upstairs to wash your hands. Breakfast is getting cold." The children jump from my grasp and follow their mother's orders like military recruits. Sierra just stands there staring at me; no, through me with her head tilted to the side as if she's waiting on me to confess something.

"What?" I ask as I try to get up from my sitting position.

Sierra pushes me back down on the mat. "Don't 'what' me, Mr. Man! You got something that you've been hiding from me, Joe? You gambling?

Getting paid off? Hit the lottery? On the take? That's what!" Sierra throws the envelope with money at my chest.

I catch it in the air with my black boxing gloves before it hits me. I remove my gloves one by one, taking a moment to organize my thoughts. I have to word this just right or Sierra is going to hit the ceiling. My best strategy is to avoid the conversation right now and try to break this dangerous news to my wife after breakfast, so not to disturb the household any more than I already have.

That's one thing about my baby; she has always trusted me to the highest degree. I should have told her about the money when I got home, but decided to let her sleep. Shit, I didn't even know what I was going to say last night, let alone today. The money must have fallen out of my back pants pocket when Sierra was straightening up the room. I've never known her to go through my pockets looking for anything. Fate is playing her hand.

How to get her to understand that I owe Chase my life? I can't tell her that I spent the night with her in Jefferson City when we were on the Missouri River Serial Killer case. We didn't make love, but we came damn close.

I look Sierra in the eyes with sincerity.
"Baby, is it possible for us to talk about this after breakfast and I promise you, it's not what you think. I couldn't do any of those things and you know that."

She still hasn't moved a muscle. Sierra shifts her body weight as she folds her arms and studies my face. "Joe, yeah, we can talk about it after breakfast as long as you tell me now where all that money came from."

"Baby, last night I went out after I got a message off call notes. I got the money from FBI Agent Royal James."

Sierra's face contorts, but she concedes and heads up stairs, leaving me with the cash standing there. I haven't seen the pissed side of her in quite a while.

I knew I was going to have to tell her, but really didn't think it would be this morning. I'm planning on leaving Sunday night, and if I had any plans on getting some lovin' before I go, well, I can just throw that right out the window.

"Damn!" I say as I head upstairs to wash my hands and have breakfast with my family.

When I sit at the table, the kids are well aware that Daddy is in trouble with Mommy. They look at both of us and I give them a half-hearted smile to let them know Daddy is on top of things. They aren't buying it.

Nia just shakes her head. "Daddy, can you say grace so we can eat?" she asks.

So much for sympathy from the children. I grasp Nia's hand; she is seated to my left. She takes Joe Jr.'s hand, who is seated next to Vernie. Sierra takes the hand of Vernie and me. As with all meals, we pray in a circle, allowing God to be the centerpiece of our home.

I bow my head and begin the Morning Prayer:

"In the name of the Father, the Son, and the Holy Spirit. God, we thank Thee for this food we are about to receive and for the nourishment of our body through Christ's sake. God bless our African ancestors, all our descendants, our family, extended family, friends, minds, bodies, and souls. God bless our heart and give us wisdom and compassion to serve Your will. Bless our enemies, and those who would wish harm upon us. Thank you, God, for all your gifts, my wife, beautiful children, and our parents. Please, God, give my father relief from his suffering, and grant him salvation when You call him to Your kingdom. Watch over our community and the world. In Your name we pray, Amen."

I finish praying. Nia says, "Dang, Daddy, why every time you in trouble you want to pray for the whole world and thangs? Can you please pass the eggs before they get cold?"

The twins both look at me and start to laugh. Sierra tilts her head the way women do when they want you to know that even the funny things ain't funny when you're holding something from them. I'm sure she just wants to get through this breakfast, so she can send the kids off to play and finish our conversation.

I push Nia playfully in the head. "Daddy's not in trouble. Why you always trying to start some mess?" I put butter and jelly on my biscuits.

"Oh, yes you are!" the twins and Sierra say in unison.

Sierra's face frowns up and she places her fork upon her plate, folds her arms, and stares at me. She has hardly touched her food. I wink at her. No response. She's concerned about my welfare. She has always been overprotective of me, but has never questioned my character or judgment. Until now.

I can't win for losing, and I'm losing my appetite very fast. I chew on a piece of bacon and decide why put off any longer what needs to be done. I'm going to have my whole family on my case, and not to mention the harassment I'll get from Vernon when he finds out what's going on.

My dad is dying of colon cancer and this thing with Agent Chase has come at a bad time. I have to be as straight as possible with everyone. This is something I have to do, even if they perceive it as selfish. I have to do this. Am I tripping or what? Chase is not worth my family. I have to try and get her out as soon as possible, because I'll never forgive myself if my Dad dies and I'm not at his side. I'll talk this out with him. He's a man of principle, so I expect him to understand. I gave my word to serve and protect, and Chase is part of the brotherhood of law enforcement.

"Daddy, we're done. Can we go play now?" Joe Jr. asks with pancake syrup on his chin.

I wipe his chin with my napkin and stroke his head. "Sure, kids. Your mom and I will be up in a minute to get your clothes and baths ready. We have to be at Grandma and Grandpa's by 2 this afternoon."

The kids rush upstairs as I help Sierra clear the breakfast table. She says nothing until I start to run the dishwater.

"Okay, Mr. Man, now that the kids are upstairs, what's all the money for? What does the FBI want you to do?" Sierra squints and tilts her head as if she's trying to look through me for an answer.

I gently take her hand and lead her to the living room sofa. This is where we have most of our discussions. With her small hands in mine I try to explain.

"Baby, when we got home last night there was a message from Cheryl Chase asking for help. She sounded very desperate, like her life depended on it."

Sierra squirms in her seat and runs her fingers through her hair and leans forward with her chin cupped within her hands. "Joe, are you sure? Did she say that her life was in danger?"

"Sierra, she would <u>not</u> call the house and leave a message like that, if she wasn't in serious peril. Anyone of us could have gotten that message. She would not be that reckless, and if there was someone else she trusted with her life, she would have called them first."

"Joe, I know Agent James would not have sent her out there alone on a case. What happened to her partner?"

I rub my right eye brow like I always do when I'm deep in thought. How to answer her without sending her into an instant panic? But Sierra is tough and God help her handle this. "FBI Agent Smelley was on assignment with her and Agent James has reason to suspect that he's met an untimely death."

Sierra jumps up. "Untimely death? Hell, Joe, can death ever be timely? What kind of crap is that? Why do they need <u>you</u> to go out in the field? There are other agents they can call on. You're a Kansas City Detective, not a Federal Bureau of Investigations Agent. Let them go after their own!" Sierra pleads while pacing the floor.

I go to her and take her in my arms. "Sierra, this is Chase we're talking about. If Agent James didn't think I could do it, he wouldn't send me. If Chase trusted anyone else, she would not have called."

Sierra looks up at me and tears form in her almond-brown eyes. "Joe, you're my husband and a father. Why do you want to risk your life for her? If it was Vernon, I'd be able to understand. He's your partner. But you don't owe these people anything."

"Baby, Chase has saved my life on at least two occasions. I wouldn't be here now if it wasn't for her."

Sierra pulls away and walks a few steps with her back to me. She pivots and stares at me intently. "Joe, do you think I'm crazy or something? I see the way Chase looks at you. She wants you. I haven't said anything to you because you haven't given me reason to, but I've always had my eye on that bitch. I don't trust the heffa."

"C'mon now, Sierra, aren't you over reacting a little?"

Sierra comes to me and cups my face with her soft honey-brown hands. "Joe, have you ever seen me over react? I'm not some stupid school kid, and neither are you. She's beautiful and she's dangerous. Why doesn't she ever bring a man with her when she comes to visit? Joe, look baby, I love you, and the kids and I need you here with us. Can't you see that?"

"Yes, I do, but I've never tried to disrespect our marriage. Sierra, you're all I need. I'll be careful, and this should be an in-and-out job. Trust me on this one." Perspiration forms on my brow.

"So how is Gertrude handling this? Is she just going to let Vernon risk his life as well?"

I turn and wipe the sweat from my forehead. This is about to get very heated. I clear my throat and announce, "Vernon isn't aware, nor is he going with me on this case." The temperature in the room goes up a hundred and four degrees.

Sierra's eyes seem to turn into marbles with the cold look she has, her nostrils are flared, and her mouth pops open, but nothing comes out. Her cheeks flush red. Her lungs seem to fill with the gasp of non-belief she has just inhaled and she yells out, "Awe, hell naw! Negro, are you crazy? You got to be kidding me, Joseph Lee Johnson!"

Sierra stands with her hands on her hips as my mother used to do. She would have the same reaction when she got irritated and upset by something I did or failed to do, and would only call my full name when thoroughly pissed to the highest of pissitivity. "Why isn't Vernon going, Joe? He's your partner. Jesus Christ, the FBI expects you to go in there <u>alone</u>?"

She throws her hands up in disgust. "I don't know if you realize it, Mr. Man, you're no Rambo or Shaft. This is suicide, Joe!"

I take her in my arms and try to calm her down. "I know I'm not some super cop, but I am good at what I do. I think on my feet and use my intelligence to get me out of situations, and that's the only way Chase will get out of there alive. Baby, try and understand. Chase is undercover with killers. Sierra, this ain't no game. She could be murdered."

"Joe, that's not our problem. I don't feel good about this. What does Chase have on you? Are you fucking her or something? Would you do this for Agent Smelley or Agent Li? This stinks, Joe. I want answers and you better not lie to me."

"Sierra, I already told you, she saved my life. To be honest, I don't know if I would do it for Smelley and Li. But Chase is a woman and it's different." Sweat forms on my brow again. Maybe it's the underlying guilt building up within me. I do like Chase, but I love my wife. I don't know if Sierra can handle the truth.

"So, you still haven't answered my question, Joe. Have you and Chase slept together?"

"Sierra, three years ago when we were on the Missouri River Serial Killer case, Chase and I had to go to Jefferson City to tell the Governor that his daughter was found dead. Agent James didn't want us to get back on the road, so we were ordered to spend the night and return the next morning. There was a Pork Convention going on and rooms were scarce. The only room that was left was one disability room, so we shared it. I have to admit I did kiss her, but nothing else happened. We came home that next morning."

Sierra slaps me across the face. "You bastard, how could you?" she says through her trembling hands that now cover her mouth as tears fill her eyes. "I trusted you, Joe."

"That's why I couldn't do anything with her. I know you love me and I would not do anything to sacrifice that, Sierra. I never had sex with Chase. I was wrong for kissing her and I swear to you, nothing has ever happened after that."

"So, you're willing to risk everything for this woman — your marriage, your children, your family, and your partner? That bitch is going to get you killed, Joe." Sierra pushes me in the chest, turns abruptly, and runs upstairs crying. The door to our bedroom slams shut.

Shit. I feel like shit on one hand for telling Sierra about Chase and I, but relieved I got that off my chest. I'll give Sierra some time alone, then try and make up.

I call Vernon and ask him to come over. He agrees as long as we shoot some hoops. I test the dishwater to make sure it's still warm and begin washing the breakfast dishes. I feel as low as a slug's butt. I've broken Sierra's trust in me and I will have to work twice as hard to get it back. This has been a long day and it's still morning.

When I finish the dishes, I inch up the stairs, trying to think of what to say to have Sierra forgive me and accept me taking this case. I understand where she is coming from. What would my own mindset be if the shoe were on the other foot.

By the time I make it to our room, the twins and Nia are consoling Sierra as she lies on the bed, crying. Joe Jr. has his thumb in his mouth and is sitting against the headboard as if he's just waiting for all this drama to be over. Nia and Vernie are on either side of their mother, already showing signs of women's solidarity. They are hugging Sierra.

Nia tells me with concern, "Daddy, Momma's sad and crying. She won't tell us what's the matter."

I pick Nia up and kiss her and address all the kids. "Well, I have to admit, children, it's Daddy's fault that Mom's crying. Daddy might have to go away for a little while and Mom's going to miss Daddy a whole bunch. But I want all of you to know that Daddy loves his family very much and you guys mean the world to me."

I put Nia down, sit next to Sierra, and put my hand softly upon her shoulder. She turns her head away from me.

Joe Jr. comes up behind me and embraces my neck. "Daddy, can I go wit' you?"

"Oh, me too," Vernie asks as she sits next to me.

Nia situates herself on my lap. "Why can't we all go, Daddy, like we do when we go on vacation?"

I swallow hard as I see the love my family has for me as Sierra sits up, wiping her face to see how I answer, and I realize what it is I'm asking my family to sacrifice. "Daddy will be working out of town. There are some bad men your Father's got to catch, and I have to help a friend out of trouble." I look Sierra in the eyes. "Daddy promises to come home safe, and I'll never take a case like this again. I just want you guys to know that I love you, and my world is nothing without all of you in it."

"How long you gonna be gone, Daddy?" Nia asks.

"Baby girl, Daddy will not be gone that long. Just long enough to take care of this business."

Sierra gathers the kids. "Come on, children, let's go make some cookies."

The kids get excited, race out of the room, and down the stairs toward the kitchen as Sierra stops in the doorway and looks at me with sorrow in her eyes. "Joe, I hope you know what you're doing." She turns and closes the bedroom door.

I lay back on the bed with my hands behind my head and pray to God that I'm making the correct decision. And for all the right reasons.

***

Vernon bursts through the door and startles me from my slumber. "What up, dawg? Damn, wake your ass up. I can't believe you didn't hear me and the kids playing downstairs. You must have some heavy shit on your mind, son." Vernon takes a bite into a homemade cookie.

The sweet chocolate smell fills the air.

"What up, Bro? I must have fallen asleep. How long you been here?" I ask as I wipe the sleep from my eyes.

"At least twenty minutes, and I been here long enough to know that Sierra is pissed about something. What you do, Nigga?" Vernon starts to work on the second and then third cookie. "Damn, these things are good," Vernon says with his mouth full as he grabs my Wilson Basketball off the floor.

"Dude, why is it that you automatically think that it was something that I did?" I ask as I pull on my tennis shoes.

Vernon tries to spin the basketball on his stubby index finger, but has never been able to do it. His efforts have improved at this point. Vernon stands around six feet and is in great shape for his age of fifty-two.

"Because Sierra is downstairs with the kids baking cookies, and you got your punk ass sitting up here in your room like she got you on punishment, that's why! Any more questions?" Vernon asks while he miserably continues to fail at spinning the ball on his finger as though he's trying to imitate a Harlem Globetrotter.

"C'mon, Vernon, why you got to be all up in my business?" I question as I head out of the room, grabbing the basketball from his grasp.

"Because that's what friends do. Make sure we stay on our partner's asses, so they'll stay on the straight and narrow," Vernon replies as he pushes me in the back toward the stairs.

Sierra is taking more cookies out the oven when Vernon and I pass though the kitchen to get to the back yard. The kids are at the table watching Fat Albert and the Cosby kids' videos while drinking milk and eating cookies. In kid heaven, they barely notice us as we pass by.

"Vernon, would you like some more cookies? There are sodas, milk, water, and juice in the refrigerator if you're thirsty," Sierra offers, never looking my way.

Vernon grabs a couple of the freshly baked cookies and puts them in a napkin.

"I don't mind if I do. Thanks, Sierra. These things are so good, you need to be selling them," Vernon says as he kisses my wife on the cheek on his way to the refrigerator.

Sierra smiles. "They're my mother's recipe, so I'd have to get permission to do that, Vernon."

"Baby, those look good. I think I'll have one myself." I reach to get a cookie from the baking tray, but Sierra moves them from my grasp. She gives me a cold stare as her smile evaporates so fast I don't even see her blink. Sierra walks toward the kitchen counter where the cookie jar is. I just stand there with my hand outreached.

"Make your own damn cookies, Mr. Selfish Man," Sierra snaps as she goes to sit with the kids at the table.

Vernon passes by me and gives me a nudge, trying to control his laughter as he heads outside. "Damn, is it getting cold in here or is it just me?" Vernon teases as he pulls the tab from the grape juice can.

I don't even bother with the cookies. It's best not to irritate my wife any more than I already have. We get on the basketball court in my driveway and Vernon comes over and puts his long arm around my shoulder.

"Joe, dang man. You got to be in some serious shit. When your woman won't even give you a cookie. You must have fucked up bad," Vernon states as he grabs the basketball from me and shoots it into the basket. "Yeah, brotha, just when you thought it couldn't get worse, Big Poppa has to come to your house and whip your ass at basketball."

"Vernon, I got this, and I can handle my wife. You just worry about this thrashing I'm about to put on your old ass, my friend."

Vernon pushes the ball into my chest. "Well dude, pull your pink panties up and take out the ball, so this old man can show you what he's working wit."

I take the ball out, fake left, then right, and drive to the basket making a lay up off the backboard. "One to nothing!"

Vernon gets the rebound and throws me the basketball. "That was luck; I dare you to do it again."

I bounce the ball in-bounds and fake to my left again, and then pull up for a fifteen-foot jumper off the glass. "Two to nothing! Where's all that shit talking you were doing?"

"Just shut up and take out, punk. That wasn't cute. You looked like Penny Hardaway on crack," Vernon jokes.

I bounce the ball in and dribble to my left, pulling up for another jump shot, which rolls around the rim, then out. Vernon grabs the rebound and puts the ball in for an easy lay up. "Here I come, baby," Vernon warns.

"Tell you what, old man; I know you ain't got no jumper no mo', so as long as you can make it from twenty feet out, I won't guard you."

"I don't need no favors because I live and die by my jumper, boy," Vernon replies as he steps in-bounds and lets fly another jump shot that falls perfectly into the hoop, causing the nets to pop.

"Hot damn, you hear that, boy? Ooh, wee! I love that sound! You better get the fire extinguisher before I burn your nets up."

"That was luck and you know it. You need to shut up, before I make you eat all that crap you talking."

Vernon steps in-bounds and lets another perfect shot fly. It goes in just like the other. "That was for your momma!"

"We playing the dozens, now? Okay then, I'm gonna give you something to tell my momma about."

Vernon steps in, but is unaware I have his rhythm down. When he goes up for another jump shot, I quickly leap and swat the ball on the roof, off the garage, and burst out laughing. "Yeah, now go and tell my momma about that, punk!"

Vernon calls out, "Foul!"

"What? Man, you must be crazy. That was all ball. You trippin', Vernon."

Vernon grabs his beefy arm, and then checks his wrist. "Joe, you are a hack. You tried to take my arm off. You were just embarrassed because I was lighting your ass up from the three-point line."

"We don't even have a three-point line. What you talking about?"

"That's what I'm saying. I was busting your butt with those thirty footers and you got jealous and lost your mind. You trying to put a brotha on injured reserve, dawg," Vernon whines, rubbing his arm.

"See, that's why I don't like playing with you. You cry worse than Magic Johnson when he was playing."

"Now, why you got to be hatin' on Magic?"

"Why you got to be lying, saying I fouled you when I blocked your shot clean?"

"Joe, why don't you just walk over there and get the ball. We'll shoot the 'mystic ball' to see who's lying, cause you know the ball never lies," Vernon reminds me.

The 'mystic ball' is how we settle arguments and bad calls. The person who makes the bad call is challenged to go to the free throw line and shoot. If he makes it, the call was a good one. If he misses, the verdict is that he was lying through his teeth.

I retrieve the ball and throw it to Vernon, who has already placed himself at the free-throw line. He bounces the ball three times and lets it fly. The shot is all net. It goes straight in.

"Liar, liar, pants on fire! I told you, you hacked the shit out of me, and you know the 'mystic ball' never lies!"

"Whatever! Your ball, Vernon." I throw Vernon the ball out of bounds, and damn if he doesn't make the next eight shots in a row.

"Fool, I told you to try and hold me and play some defense. You don't think fat meat is greasy," Vernon says, grinning from ear to ear.

"Dude, I let you win. Shut up!" I say, laughing. Then my laughter dies. "Vernon, I need to talk to you."

Vernon frowns, "This about you and Sierra?"

I place the basketball between my legs, sit on top of it, and look up. "Yeah, but it has to do with you as well."

"Joe, is this gonna be one of those cigar moments?" Which he does when he's about to hear something he isn't going to like.

Vernon rubs his well-manicured hand over his close cropped head.

"Yep, you might as well go get it now, Vernon."

My friend gives me a curious look and heads to the driveway for one of his cigars. Vernon always puts a cigar in his mouth when he's nervous, serious, or about to get violent. I know my partner and he's not going to like what I have to tell him one bit.

Vernon strolls back up the driveway, takes a seat on the step leading to the backdoor of the house, and places his cigar in his wide mouth. He never lights it; he just chews on it. "All right boy, you got me out here. What's on your mind?"

I get up and throw Vernon the ball, which he places under his arm. I pull up one of the lawn chairs and sit across from him.

"Vernon, Chase is deep undercover on a case that involves dirty cops killing drug dealers for money. They're also killing cops who try to get out of the organization. Chase has gotten in next to the head guy, some Cuban named Dread Cattanno. He's a Police Sergeant for the Nebraska Police Department. He's been under suspicion for a while, but they haven't been able to bust this guy. Agent James gave me the case file. He also has reason to believe that Agent Smelley is dead."

Vernon sits back in his chair and his brown skin seems to get darker as his eyes narrows. "Damn, Joe. This sounds like some serious shit. If Smelley got his cover blown, Chase is on borrowed time."

"Exactly! So, something has to be done. And fast."

Vernon scrunches up his wide nose. "Joe, what the hell we know about Nebraska?"

"Vernon, it doesn't stop there. This guy got connections and is operating in Oklahoma, Iowa, Nebraska, and Kansas. They call it a 'Black Ring'. Dirty cops killing to get rich."

"Shit, what're we gonna do for back up? We won't know what cops to trust and who's dirty? I know a few guys in the other departments, but not good enough to rely on their information." Vernon twirls the cigar in his mouth.

I decide not to tell him about the front money, because he might think I'm doing it just for that. And I can't let him think that he's in on this. I can put my own life in jeopardy, but not Vernon's. Not this time.

"Vernon, Agent James asked me to take this case and I agreed to. Solo!

I'll be leaving Sunday."

Vernon starts to laugh. "Stop fucking around, Joe. You never know when to take shit serious."

"But, I am serious, Vernon. I can't ask you to do this. Chase and I have history, and I owe her my life."

Vernon stands with the ball under his arm, bites down on his cigar, and then grabs it out of his mouth. "We got history, Joe. I'm your partner, remember? I owe you my life and my wife's. How you expect to do this alone?"

I rub my right eye-brow. "Agent James will assist me with cooperatives, and I was going to call on a couple of friends that grew up with me and Pretty Kevin."

"Damn, Joe, you're going to trust your life with a pimp? What kind of crazy shit is that?"

"Vernon, Kevin has given that life up for two years now. Why you always giving Pretty Kevin a hard time?"

I grew up and went to college with Kevin. He got caught up in the Missouri River Serial Killer case when his prostitutes started coming up missing and their dead bodies were found floating in the river. He was a prime suspect, but we ended up solving the case and Kevin was cleared. He now is part-owner of Ebony Plastics, which is doing very well. Making over five million dollars per year.

Vernon slaps his knees. "Shit, Joe, this ain't about Kevin. This is about my so-called partner making decisions without me. That's not how it's supposed to work. Our shit is about trust, honor, and respect. Not selfish decisions that can get you killed. This is about friendship, man."

"That's why I'm not getting you involved, Vernon. Man, Gertrude would never forgive me if something happened to you. Pretty Kevin can hook me up with Mo-Mo and St. Louis Slim. These guys love this kind of dangerous shit and I know they'll have my back. They both owe me big time, and it's time for them to pay up. Vernon, you know Commissioner Wayne ain't going to let both of us do this. Look at the caseload we already got. You got to stay and cover for me. You got to look after my wife and kids while I'm gone, man. Who else can I trust to do that, Bro?"

"Joe, Mo-Mo and St. Louis Slim are going to get you killed. Both them niggas are crazy and you know it."

"Yeah, but both are very loyal and got friends in shady places all over the six-state area. I can get guns and good information from the underground black market that they both deal in."

Vernon sits back on the step and gives a heavy sigh. "Joe, why you doing this? You been fucking around with Chase or something?" Vernon puts his cigar back into his mouth.

"Naw, Vernon. I kissed her one time, but I never had her, dawg."

"Yeah right, Nigga. That's bullshit, Joe!"

I rub my right eye-brow and look Vernon in the eyes. "Vernon, I've never lied to you, man. I ain't gonna start now."

"Whatever, dude. This is fucked up. No wonder your wife is pissed. You're willing to lose your woman over this? Has this been cleared with Commissioner Wayne, Joe?"

"Agent James is clearing it with him. I go pick up my car from the impound at FBI headquarters on Sunday."

"Joe, what about your dad? Your pops can go any day now. Are you willing to deal with the guilt if he passes before you get back? You know that would kill your mom."

"Why you got to bring that shit up, Vernon?"

Vernon walks up to me and takes his cigar out of his mouth, standing so close that the sweet tobacco on his breath hits me in the face.

"Because these are the facts and this is real, Joe. A lot of people will be affected if something happens to you. Have you even thought of your children? Have you checked out everything? Something just ain't right about this shit, Joe. You got a lot to lose, if this stuff goes wrong." Vernon grips my shoulders and stares deep in my eyes.

"What about Chase, Vernon? Should I just sit back and do nothing and let her die?"

"Let the FBI handle it, Joe."

I grab the back of my neck. "Vernon, you don't understand. I already took the case. Agent James gave me $50,000.00 for front money. It's upstairs in my dresser drawer. I got to do this."

"Return the money, Joe. You ain't got to do shit."

"I'm a cop, Vernon. Chase needs me and I owe her."

"Well, I see you got this shit in your head, so fuck me and what I think. Right, partner?" Vernon shoves the basketball in my chest, looks at me, shakes his head, and walks to his car and drives off.

Vernon has never acted like this. Will our friendship ever be repaired? I turn to go in the house and Sierra is in the doorway with tears in her eyes. She must have heard the whole thing. I sit on the steps and put my head in my hands.

I have to trust my gut feeling on this, but I'm hurting so many people I love in the process. Am I that selfish? Why am I willing to sacrifice so much? It's my job and I owe Chase my life and she would do it for me. This has been the hardest thing I've done, and yet, it will be harder explaining this to my mom and dad. My dad is dying of cancer, and I will use all the resources possible to get back to Kansas City as fast as I can.

I'll have to call St. Louis Slim and Mo-Mo to set up a meeting. They'll have my back even though St. Louis Slim still hasn't gotten over our last argument, but I know he won't hold that against me. At least, I hope not.

four

CHASE WAKES UP IN A HOTEL ROOM, SORE ALL OVER WITH THE SOUR taste of congealed blood in her mouth. She struggles to rise from the bed and wonders how they got her in there unconscious. Did they walk her through a lobby, or did one of Dread's henchmen pay one of the hotel workers so they could sneak her up a back entrance, on some freight elevator away from any suspecting hotel guests?

By the Christopherian furnishings, she gathers that this place is very expensive. It must be a suite. Shadows of feet move under the door. Television noise and conversation come from the next room. Her room is dark, but the shades are pulled back enough for the moon to gaze in. She remembers her mom calling the moon God's night light. It sheds enough light for her to find her way to the bathroom without tripping over her overnight bag.

Chase pulls her bag into the bathroom with some difficulty, close the door, and without thinking switch on the light. She's immediately blinded by the bright fluorescent lights that illuminate the larger-than-usual area. When her equilibrium and sight adjusts to the lighting, she's surprised that her encounter with Brutus didn't leave her as badly bruised as she's feeling.

A slight bruise swells on her right cheek, and her lip is a little swollen on her right side as well. She's glad her arm blocked her face. Too bad it didn't block the cuts on the inside of her mouth. She runs her tongue in her mouth to check for any loose teeth. They're fine. Brutus could have hurt her worse, and she counts her blessings that he considers her a friend. She'll have to let him make the first move next time. It was silly for her to get caught in the air. She knew better.

Her face has a light coating of dust, as do her hair and clothes. She pulls some straw from under her shirt and suddenly feels weak kneed as she thinks of Agent Smelley swinging from that rope, gutted like a hog. At least Dread didn't burn his body as he did all the others. She pushes the tears back and vows to get even. She has to be smart and keep a cool head. She has to contact her superior, FBI Agent Royal James, and let him know of her position.

She looks around the gold-toned bathroom with the oversized French marble Jacuzzi, bathtub, and vanity. By the wall, off from the freestanding shower is a wall phone. Thank God for hotels. Chase is surprised to find that the information on the phone reveals that they are at the Downtown Hyatt Regency hotel in Sioux City, Iowa, room number 1611. She looks out the door to make sure no one has entered the room. She pulls out her small cell phone and mutes the sound. She carefully dials Agent Jame's cell phone number.

It rings two times. "James' here."

She whispers into the phone. "This is Chase."

Agent James's pitch rises immediately. "Chase, are you all right? Where the hell are you? We got to get you out; we believe we've found Agent Smelley. He's been burned."

"Agent James, I fear for my life, but I'm okay. Agent Smelley was not burned he was killed in Nebraska. His body is in a red barn that's on a deserted dirt country road near Freemont, just off Highway 30. Dread killed him. He cut him up something awful." Her voice breaks.

Agent James pauses for a moment. "Chase, we thought we had Smelly's body here. Some poor bastard has been burned to a crisp and he's about the same size as Smelly. You got to get out of there."

"That was Officer Paul Novesell. He double crossed Dread on a drug bust, and tried to keep part of the money for himself. Dread had him killed and burned. If I see the opportunity, I'll get out. They have someone watching me constantly. There are at least six men with Dread at all times."

"Joe should be on his way to help you get out. Just hang tough and stay alive until he can get to you. Where are you?"

"Thank God. I'm in Sioux City…" The door to her room opens and she flips the phone shut and shoves it in her panties. That is one place they won't search.

Dread enters the bathroom. He has on a black leather shirt and pants outfit with red snakeskin boots and belt. His eyes become slits as he canvasses the room suspiciously. Chase tries to put on her best mean and tough face that she can muster.

"You see what Brutus did to my face? I feel like shit and I need to take a shower. Do you mind?"

Dread walks up behind her and wraps his arms around her body as he pins her to the vanity. His penis bulges against her behind. They stare at each other through the reflection in the mirror.

"Yes, I mind! I didn't mean for you to get hurt, but you made my boys look bad, no? Oh, you excited me da way you handled yourself. I just want to make sure that you are okay, and I ask for your forgiveness, dear. Can't we make passionate love and make up?" Dread presses harder and harder against her, his breathing growing heavier.

He places his hands on her buttocks and starts to grind. As his intensity gets faster, Chase pushes back, turns to face him, and slaps his face. "I will not be treated like a twenty-dollar whore, Dread. My body is sore all over, I'm dirty and not in the mood to be mauled or manhandled!"

Dread throws his hands up in a surrendering motion while giving her an amused smile. "Please excuse me. You are right. I am beside myself. I will leave you to get dressed. We have another meeting in three hours.

That should give you time to freshen up and get dressed." Dread adjusts his penis into his pants and gathers himself. He slicks back his jet-black hair, wipes the sweat from his brow, adjusts his clothes, and takes a deep breath.

He blows her a kiss as he pulls the bathroom door shut. Chase puts her ear to the wooden door just long enough to hear the bedroom door close. She goes into the bedroom to make sure he has exited. The room is vacant. She can still hear the men laughing and talking in the other room.

She falls upon the bed and breaths a sigh of relief as she retrieves her cell phone from her underwear and tries to call Agent James back. His line is busy. She tries two more times, and returns the cell phone to her purse, frowning. He should have been expecting her to call back. She tries to convince herself that he's contacting Joe and letting him know she's at some hotel in Iowa.

Two hours later she finds herself in the back of the black sport utility vehicle with Dread sitting next to her. They are to meet with one of Dread's supporters. Dread usually doesn't get involved in the collection of money that is owed, but in this case, he explained that Iowa Police Officer Christopher O'Brian has been skimming the profits in the amount of forty thousand dollars in the last two months. Dread wants to make an example of this guy.

An example for Dread always ends up in someone being killed. He is serious about his money and loyalty. Chase hasn't met this O'Brian guy, but he has to be a fool to steal from Dread. If she knew how sinister this guy was before she took the case, she wouldn't have gotten into it. She hates being in these situations where Dread is handling his business; they're more like executions than examples.

She stares out the SUV's window into the starlit, country night and wonders about her fate. She opens the window a bit and breaths in deeply the cool, sweet, country, night air and almost forgets the danger. She says a silent prayer that she comes out of this assignment alive.

They pull into Moville, Iowa, a small and rustic town. It looks like

Mayberry by the white-picket-fence houses. A big oak tree sits in the middle of the town square as they pass the jailhouse.

Is Otis in his cell drunk with his cow grazing behind the jailhouse? Are Barney and Andy inside drinking coffee and explaining life lessons to Opey and Goober? They quickly pass through the tiny town and pull off a road that leads to a sprawling field. Chase spots the Sioux City, Iowa police vehicle as they pull on either side of it.

"Chase, you stay here. I'll be right back." Dread kisses her on the cheek, and before she can answer, he gets out of the car with Brutus, Weasel, and Ronnell.

Officer O'Brian gets out of his police cruiser with his palms exposed as he greets Dread. O'Brian is on the overweight side with a carrot top and freckles that cover his broad face. He looks like he could have played football at one time, but gave up his dream and settled for fried Hostess Twinkies, two at a time.

He stands about five feet, ten inches, with a childish face and stubby fingers. Dread looks disgustingly at him. Chase lets her window down so she can hear the conversation. The night air has dropped at least twenty degrees, and puffs of smoke come as the men speak.

She fidgets. It would be foolish for O'Brian to come out to this deserted place alone. She surveys the grounds. Something moves just beyond the clearing. The high three-quarter moon illuminates our surroundings.

The high prairie grass, about three to four feet high, dances in the night wind. She pulls the Smith and Wesson .44 Magnum pistol that Dread keeps in a secret compartment behind the backseat arm rest and grab two bullet clips. Checking the clip in the gun to make sure it is full, she slaps it back into the handle, and then pulls the slide back, loading a bullet into the chamber.

Chase reaches up and turns off the dome light and push the car door ajar, just in case something goes down. She tunes back in on the conversation of Dread and O'Brian, but remains on high alert, surveying the landscape for any intruders.

Dread is smiling while grabbing the back of his neck. Always a bad sign. He only does this when stressed.

"So, O'Brian, I haven't taken good care of you for handling my Iowa accounts?"

"Yes, Dread, you have. Very well. I have your money right here." O'Brian opens his uniform shirt, which reveals his bullet-proof vest. He pulls three stacks of cash from underneath it and hands it to Dread. Dread looks at Adam, another Nebraska police officer, who handles the books for his organization.

The White guy with blond hair, a medium muscular build, and looks a little like Ben Affleck, he takes the money, fingers through it quickly, and shakes his head. Then he quickly steps back with the other three men, Clark, Christopher, and Damon, who have escorted us.

Dread claps his hands and laughs. "It tis' getting cold out here, is it not?"

"It's been colder," O'Brian answers as he buttons his shirt. His hands are shaking.

"Yes, colder. Cold can be an anomaly. Like when life is escaping your body, they say dat you feel cold all over." Dread looks O'Brian in the eyes. "Have you heard that?"

"No, I'm not much interested in dying or what happens to dead people," O'Brian replies as he looks around at Dread's men, who have formed a wide circle encompassing him. O'Brian's eyes dart between the men as if he's looking for an escape route. His eyes bulge with fear.

"No? Well, it seems you would be after thinking that you could steal from me, you fucking maggot?" Dread snaps.

"I don't know what you're talking about. I've always paid you on time," O'Brian responds, taking a step backward.

Dread takes a step forward.

"No, my friend. To our calculations, you are about... how much, Adam?" Dread looks over at his accountant.

"Fifty-thousand to this point!" Adam answers.

"Fifty-thousand," Dread echoes as he turns back to the Sioux City, Iowa Policeman.

O'Brian points up at the moon. "Well, I guess all good things come to an end, and it looks like a good night for dying," he says with a smirk.

This time she knows she hears something moving through the tall grass. She ducks down in the seat as several men pass the vehicle and surround Dread and his men with their rifles and shotguns drawn, before Dread's guys reach for their weapons.

Chase weighs her options. Drive off and leave Dread and his men at the fate of the redneck countrymen? But, if Dread were to make it out of the situation alive... She also thinks of the good old boys shooting out her tires, and can only imagine what they would do to her before killing her. She plays the odds and decides to stick around and help out Dread and his men.

"Well, isn't this cozy," O'Brian says. You think I'm some kind of fool? Why should I let some fucking Cuban make all the money? I see it like this: I run this territory and get twenty percent off the top, or I get it all. There's no negotiation, so you can just jump your Cuban Black ass back in your SUV and get your punk asses out of my town. I'll mail you your money from here on out. You got a problem with that, Cubie?" O'Brian asks with his gun pointed at Dread's scrotum.

Dread sees Chase sneaking up on one of O'Brian's men, gun aimed at his head. "Actually, yes. I do have a serious problem with dat."

She pushes the Magnum against the skull of the shotgun-toting hick. "Drop your weapons now or I'll blow his brains out!" She orders.

By this time, Dread has disarms O'Brian to his amazement, and holds the gun to O'Brian's scrotum. The other six men quickly drop their weapons and raise their hands as Dread's men huddle them together.

Dread motions her over to him. "You never cease to amaze me. I'm sorry dat I doubted your loyalty." He kisses her on the cheek and turns back to O'Brian. "See, dat is loyalty. It takes a woman to show you how to act, and she will be rewarded handsomely. Adam, how much we got there in cash?"

Adam quickly calculates the money he has already put in a black duffle bag. "About sixty-five thousand, boss."

Dread orders to her astonishment, "Give it to Chase. That's for you, baby, and I hope it makes up for the pain you had to endure for my mistrust."

"It more than makes up for it, Dread. Thanks!" She replies as Adam hands Chase the dusty duffle bag.

Dread smiles and winks at Chase. "Okay, baby, can you go wait in the car for us? I think it's about to get ugly around here."

"Sure, baby," she answers, not wanting to watch the carnage that is sure to follow. She throws the dirty black money bag in the SUV, but doesn't get in. Her curiosity of what Dread will do to the betrayers has gotten the best of her, and she will have to give an eye-witness account in detail of the deeds done, if the case ever gets to trial.

The redneck's raunchy body odor and perspiration from fear fills the air as the six men are forced to their knees. A gunshot sounds. O'Brian grabs between his legs, screaming as he falls to his knees, then collapse onto the grass as his khaki police pants darken with blood and country dirt.

"What's da fucking problem, maggot? You da' one like to point guns at people's balls. I figure you like dat feeling?" Dread mocks, laughing. "Pick his punk ass up and throw him in his car and get the petro," Dread orders.

Christopher and Adam grab O'Brian and place him in his vehicle as he whimpers.

Clark goes to the back of the SUV, grabs the gas can, and rushes to stand next to the driver's side of O'Brian's squad car. Smiling, he does not hesitate to open the can and place the spout upright, so the gasoline can be poured out.

The Iowa hicks kneeling on the ground join in the whimpering and start to plead with Dread for mercy. One urinates on himself as he shakes with fear, and tears stream down his face.

"Mercy, you say? How much mercy would you have on me and my men, you piece of shit?" Dread spits at the three hundred and fifty-pound, cow-faced man. "What we gonna have here is a little barbecue. Then I'm gonna give you boys a fair shake, okay?" Dread explains with an honest smile.

O'Brian face is contorted as he looks over at Dread in obvious pain. "Dread, I got your money. Look in the bag in the trunk."

O'Brian pops the trunk from the inside as Christopher pushes his gun into O'Brian's temple.

Brutus starts toward the trunk to retrieve the money.

"No, Brutus, you stay there and cover those assholes. Clark, get the money."

Clark takes a flashlight out of his jacket, and walks toward the trunk. He retrieves a duffel bag, lays it on the ground, opens it, then screams. A five-foot rattlesnake jumps out and strikes him in the face. He falls backward and struggles with the big snake that refuses to let go of its bite.

Brutus pulls his switchblade, grabs the head of the huge snake, and cuts the body from it. He carefully pulls the head from Clark's face. But Clark has already gone into shock and convulsions from the snake's poison.

Brutus shoots Clark in the head to take him out of his misery as blood squirts profusely from his face. Brutus goes over and kicks the duffel bag, then dumps multiple large bundles of hundred dollar bills.

Dread clenches his fist, spits at the ground and kicks the car door several times in a rage. He looks at Clark, and then at O'Brian, who wears a smirk.

"It should have been you, you Cuban bastard!" O'Brian yells.

Dread slowly goes over and punches him in the face repeatedly, then grabs the gas can from the ground, and pours it all over O'Brian and inside the vehicle. O'Brian tries to yank the can from Dread, but gets a quick elbow to the face each time he tries.

O'Brian pleads, "Please don't do this. You got the money. For heaven's sake, just shoot me!"

Dread lights a match and flicks it into the police car. Fire engulfs the vehicle. The metallic smell of gasoline and the rotten egg smell of burning flesh fill the night air along with the screams of O'Brian.

He tries to get out of the car, but is shot in the shoulder by Dread as he kicks the door shut. One last bellowing yell comes as O'Brian gives in to his living hell. "Jesus, help me!"

His skin melts with his clothing as the once pale, red haired, countrified man is nothing more than a charred hunk of black flesh with his teeth protruding form his black charred face.

Dread picks up the twitching body of the rattlesnake and tosses it into the burning vehicle.

"Shit ain't funny no more, eh asshole?" Dread asks the burned body.

He slicks back his black hair and takes a deep breath, then turns to the horrified men kneeling on the ground. He motions for his men to get behind them.

"Okay, I'm a gonna tell you what I am gonna do for you assholes. We gonna count to ten, and if you fat maggots can out run a bullet, you live. Or you can stay knelling and die not trying. Anybody got a problem wit' dat?" Dread raises his gun to the level of their heads. No one answers.

Dread counts to ten, and the six men get up screaming as chaos unfolds. They begin running for their lives into the field. Dread and his men open fire, dropping all six.

Dread motions to Ronnell and Weasel to go and make sure they are all dead. They walk into the fields with their flashlights. A shot can be heard here and there until all the men have been accounted for, and they return putting their guns away.

The group collects the money that has been dumped on the ground, and then they come to the vehicles.

"I thought I told you to get in the van?" Dread asks.

Chase was lost for words. Dread was not bothered in the least. She climbed into the back seat and rests her head on the headrest and tries to push back the memory of what she witnessed.

Dread and his men get into the SUV's, and slowly drive off as they had entered the barren place. The fire from O'Brian's squad car illuminates the mid-night sky.

five

THIS RIDE TO MOM'S AND DAD'S HOUSE IS THE FIRST TIME THAT Sierra and I have nothing to say to each other. I can not find the words to start a conversation, and Sierra just looks out the window and gives me an occasional snide glance.

The kids are as jovial as ever. Thank God, that they can forgive me so fast. The twins of course just want their needs met. As long as Daddy or Mommy is around to play, feed them, and wash them when they are dirty, they are cool. The children get unconditional love and time, and are basically spoiled rotten by their grandparents and us. Life is good.

I already know that by the time we let the kids out and make it to the front door of my parents' house, that this will be the most agonizing of all my explanations. My dad and I are best friends. I am the baby of fifteen children. Mom was a widow and had five children when she married my widower father, who had five kids of his own.

Their blessed union was the source of five additional children. We have five girls and ten boys, and I am the last of the group, number fifteen. Our family never referred to each other as "step-children." Our parents would not allow it. They demanded and were examples of sacrifice and love. The younger child could never strike a child older. That was the rule, and Mom and Dad enforced it.

I was tortured quite often, and learned the art of manipulation and extortion early in life. It was my balance and the only chance of survival at the hands of my older, tough brothers. A quick wit would get you everywhere, and a tattletale would get you beat up when our parents weren't around.

We had plenty of fun, too, and created all sorts of games. We would put on talent shows and dance contests with Mom and Dad being the judges, but they often joined in on the fun.

It was so cool having both parents and I didn't realize until I was older, just how important that was. Most of the other kids on my block came from one-parent homes. Our parents have been married for fifty-two years, and it doesn't look like Dad will make it to his fifty-third wedding anniversary.

It was weird when the doctor at Research Medical Center called us in for a family gathering to discuss Dad's cancer. He told us that Dad had two to three weeks to live, and asked if we wanted him placed in an Assisted Living Center, or would we prefer that he retire at home. I always associated retirement with work, not life and death.

While in the meeting, my dad called for my mom and me, and the nurse came in and got us. Dad is a pretty sharp fellow, and after seeing so many of us at the hospital at the same time, he knew something bad was up.

When Mom and I entered the room, my father was already questioning us. My mom couldn't take it, broke down crying, and left the room. She could not lie to my dad. So it was just him and me. My father is my buddy and my life-long hero.

"Give it to me straight, boy," my dad ordered, looking me in the eyes. My father looked up at the ceiling as though preparing himself for bad news and looking into the heavens would secure his soul. His eyes watered, but my dad trusted me to tell him the truth.

"Dad, they're giving you about two to three weeks to live. The cancer is terminal. They say your white blood cells are growing more rapidly than your red, and there is nothing they can do at this point, but make you comfortable. They asked if you want to go into an Assisted Living Home or go back to the house.

Dad smiled at me, wiped a tear from his eye, and took my hand. "Hell, I ain't seen my grandbabies the week I've been in this place. I want to go home and spend some time with my family and grandbabies."

I hugged my dad and we both began to cry. Not tears of loss, but tears of pride. Twelve years earlier, my dad, who was a functioning alcoholic and smoked two packs of Camel cigarettes a day, gave up both smoking and drinking at the same time. What strength, discipline, and courage it took to do that.

My pops raised fifteen children and never considered leaving us alone. No surprise that when death is certain, he thinks of his family and grandbabies. I always admired my father, but now our bond can only grow deeper. Please God let the doctor be wrong. But thank you that I am the offspring of such a wonderful man.

My sister, Candice, who has come to stay with my parents and help out during this trying time, greets us at the door. Three of my brothers jump from their seats in the living room to say hello. John, Aaron, and Paul each grab a child, and then we exchange hugs.

"Where's Mom?" I ask, looking around the living room.

"She's in her room. She's been really depressed seeing dad in his condition," John answers as the kids run into the kitchen to get some of the sweets my sisters have baked.

"And how's Dad?" Sierra asks as she puts her hand on my shoulder. This is a natural reaction for her, no matter the rest of the circumstances.

With tears in his eyes, my other brother, Ronald who has just come from upstairs answers, "He's not doing so well. He's kind of in and out of it. I've never seen Dad this weak before. It's really hard."

Sierra and I both reach for my brother and hug him. He wipes his eyes as John takes him outside to get some air, so not to upset the children.

I turn and hug my wife. "Sierra, I just want you to know how much I love you. I know you're upset with me right now, but I really appreciate what you've meant to me all these years. I just want you to know that."

"Joe, you mean the world to me, and I would die if something happened to you. You're my man, and I'll be damned if I'm gonna let some other woman take you from me," Sierra says as she pulls me to her and holds me tight.

"Baby, that's something that will never happen. You're all the woman I need. Believe that. Let's go check on my parents." I kiss my wife softly and take her hand as we ascend the oak staircase to the second floor of the three-story house.

In my parents' room, Mom is sitting at my father's side, holding his hand while they watch television.

"Hello, children. I didn't hear you guys come in," Mom says as she rises to greet us. Her eyes are puffy and red. She is happy to see us, but you can tell she is weary and tired, but still wears a smile. My mom is a full-figured, beautiful pecan-brown-skinned woman, with medium-length hair that reveals her Indian bloodline. A deep, spiritual woman who always places her family first, she is an excellent mother and wife. My dad adores her. And she adores him.

"Hi, Dad," Sierra says as she hugs and kisses my father.

"Hey, girl, how are you doing? I would get up to greet you, but this old man is tired today, and I can't seem to get this pain under control," Dad says as he sits up in the bed. He's grimaces from pain, but his pride and gentlemanly ways give him enough strength to push himself up into a sitting position. Mom and Sierra place pillows behind his back.

"Baby, you be careful now. Take your time," Mom exclaims as she fusses over Dad.

"I'm okay, I just got to catch my breath." Dad looks over at me as I marvel at his strength and pride. "Damn boy, you gonna just stand there and stare at me or are you gonna come over here and show your old man some love?" Dad opens his thin arms and smiles, waiting on my embrace.

I hug my dad and tears just flow from my eyes.

"I love you so much, Dad, and I wish it was me instead of you in that bed," I say.

Dad pushes me back and looks me in the eye. "Boy, I wouldn't wish this cancer on anybody. I've lived a full life and I've been blessed with fifteen children, a beautiful wife, and a shit load of grandchildren. I hope that your life will be as full as mine has…and I ain't dead yet, so let's dry all these here tears up and you tell me what you been doing?"

"Mom, let's go get us a cup of coffee," Sierra suggests after my mom starts to cry. Tears fill my eyes as well.

"Boy, don't be getting wet-eyed on my account. The Lord's been good to me. Sierra, y'all send my grandkids up here, so I can get my sugar. I want to see my grandbabies," Dad explains as he wipes his eyes and blows his nose.

I take the seat in the chair next to Dad after Sierra and Mom leave. My brothers John, Ronald, Aaron, and Paul enter and stand around by the oak dresser across from Dad's bed, waiting to participate in the conversation that has yet to take place.

"It's good seeing you up, Dad. Seems like you're feeling better," my brother John says.

He flew in from San Francisco, California four days earlier. He's a retired Master Chief with the United States Air Force. He is meticulous about time and having a routine for everything. You can set your watch and calendar by him. He sometimes forgets he's out of the military and has a tendency to order us younger brothers around, but we always playfully remind him about it.

"So Joe, what's this Sierra tells us about some case you're about to take?" Paul asks.

Paul has had some bouts with crack and is continually trying to get his life back together. I often tease him of being over-fifty without benefits. A disabled vet after being shot in the shoulder in the Vietnam War. He has not had a steady job in five years.

My brother was a pimp after the war, and I think he is still chasing his past, and what he has lost due to drugs. He is funny and talented, but his demons keep pulling him back into the life of misery. Our family will not stop loving him or give up on him, though.

I explain to them the case I'm about to take on, the circumstances behind my decision to take the case, and how Vernon feels about it. Dad says nothing, but rubs his head and gives me an uneasy glance.

My brother Aaron is a big man, weighing around two-hundred and eighty pounds, all muscle. He's a handsome man, chocolate in complexion, balding with a graying beard to match his age of fifty-five years. "Damn, Joe, my wife would never go for some shit like that. You got to be out of your mind. I know Sierra is pissed about it. Shit, it's making me mad and I ain't even married to your selfish ass."

"Look, I owe this woman my life on a couple of occasions. And this isn't about me being selfish. It's about me saving a friend. And aren't you the same person that has to ask his wife for permission just to take out the trash? Your woman won't even let you come to my house without checking up on you, so you need to stop tripping with me. She probably got on your underwear as we speak." We all start to laugh at my brother's expense. It lightens the room for a moment.

"Well, you say what you want, but I wear the drawers in my house," Aaron says puffing out his chest.

"Yeah, but who wears the drawers outside of the house?" I question with a goofy look on my face to add to the mockery. "Aren't you the same person that tried to be funny and pay your ex-wife her first alimony payment of seven hundred dollars in pennies?" I interrogate.

My brother shifts his weight and frowns as the rest of us smile.

"Why you always got to be pulling that out your ass, Joe? That judge had no right having me pay alimony to Jeanette. She made more money than I did. It pissed me off, so I got one of my boys and we went around to all the banks and got the pennies." He rubs his fingers together as he walks up to John and he continues his story. "I got two of those tin, silver-colored trashcans with the lids and put a big red ribbon on them. Then I filled them with seventy thousand pennies and sat them on the front porch with a note inside that said, 'the first of three alimony payments' I would have loved to see the look on her face. I bet she probably shit on herself." He starts to laugh, and I have to admit, the act was so conniving and stupid that it's funny.

Dad grins, "Well, that wasn't so funny when that judge locked your ass up in jail with those trashcans full of seventy thousand pennies and made you stay in jail until you had rolled those pennies up into seven hundred penny rolls. It took you two days to get it done. Now <u>that</u> was funny!" Dad laughs as we join in.

Aaron shakes his bald graying head. "Man, y'all just don't know how close I came to killing that woman. I rolled so many pennies that I couldn't think straight. Sometimes when I would lose count, I would just call out her name. Man, every time I saw a loose penny on the ground I had thoughts of going over to her house and just strangling the shit out of her. I thought I was gonna need therapy. That was a stressful time."

I go over and put my arm around his shoulders. "Now why should I listen to a man who would pull a stunt like that? Your current wife has you so hen-pecked she probably doesn't even let you wear underwear, unless she picks them out," I tease.

My brother unbuttons his coveralls and reveals his boxer shorts, which have little butterflies on them. We all just roll out laughing, and Dad laughs so hard he starts to cough.

"Y'all go head and laugh. These are the type of underwear that drives women crazy. Makes your woman call you 'Big Poppa'," Aaron says, grinning as we burst into laughter again.

I have to give Dad a glass of water to help stop his coughing from the laughter.

My brother John walks over to me, "Joe, you need to make sure you get a good understanding with your woman and your partner, before you leave. Relationships built on trust, can only stay solid if that trust is solidified and shared." John sits on Dad's bed and continues, "Don't cut your partner out; let him make a decision for himself. Your wife has enough to worry about with you on the case. Don't let her mind start to wonder about your conviction. Let her know you love her, and that she's first in your life. I've been in the military a long time, and my wife has had to pick up and move whenever I got relocated. So whenever possible, I made extra sacrifices to make sure she was happy. I told her everyday how much I appreciated her and showed her as well. You got a good woman; I'd hate for you to risk losing her."

I rub my eye brow and chew on my bottom lip. Am I really being selfish? I'll talk to Vernon and Sierra again and hopefully we can come to some happy medium.

My brother Paul has his hair licked back in curly waves. We tease him that's it's the result of an S-curl, but he denies it. He is of deep brown complexion with a smile like a horse, due to all his back teeth being pulled. "What about Dad, Joe? How long will you be gone? We don't know the day or the hours. What if something happens? Will you be able to forgive yourself for not being here?" The once jovial mood comes to a screeching halt.

Dad looks at Paul and shakes his head. "Paul, I'll be here awhile. You don't put that on Joe's shoulder. He has a dangerous case he has to be on, and he doesn't need any shit like that on his conscious. Damn, I can't believe you. Joe, you follow your heart. This is your decision to make. Take into consideration what John told you, because that's good advice."

Dad pauses to take a drink of water and continues, "But you take care of yourself, and if you do decide to go save Agent Chase, you make sure you don't take any unnecessary chances. Vernon and Sierra will understand. They are your best friends and they will be by your side. Now, all y'all come over here and let's pray," Dad orders as he makes the sign of the cross.

"In the name of the Father, the Son, and the Holy Spirit. Dear Lord, bless my family and my wife. Bless all my children's families and their extended families. Let

not their hearts be troubled when I enter into Your glory. I know You have prepared a place for me in the kingdom of heaven and would not put me through anything on this earth that I can't handle. Protect my children and keep them safe from harm. Send Your angels to help them make sound decisions and ward off the devils of drugs, negativity, and laziness. Bless my grandbabies and let their lives be full of happiness and love. Jesus, keep anointing my beautiful wife, and let not her heart be burdened. Temper my pain, Lord, that I may have a smooth transition to the other side that I may meet my family and ancestors that have gone before me to Your land of eternal bliss. In this I pray, Amen."

We all hug our dad and solemnly kiss him on his forehead. There is a rumble of tiny feet coming up the stairs and children giggling as Dad grasps my hand before I clear a way for them to get to their granddad. He looks at me and as he smiles.

"Joe, follow your heart, mind, and soul and they will not lead you wrong. Do what you feel you must do. You won't be able to live with yourself if you don't. If everyone loves you as they say, they will love you when you return. It won't be easy, but it will work out." Dad releases my hand as the kids run to his side.

"We brought you some jellybeans from downstairs, grandpa. We picked out the black ones cause' we know you don't eat those," Nia says as Vernie and Joe Jr. nod.

"Okay, boys, it's the grandkids' turn. Y'all leave me with my grandchildren," Dad orders, his face aglow as he gets kisses and hugs from the kids. They feed him jellybeans and he smiles and laughs with my three children. He's stronger now. I have to admit, I wish that I'll be loved the way he is when I'm his age.

We descend the stairs, and I go to my wife, hug her from behind, and kiss her softly on her neck.

Mom says, "Well, that's my cue to go see about my husband and grandbabies. I'll see you two later. Joe, be there for your wife, son. Don't hurt her; cherish her. She loves you too much to be upset the way she is." Mom kisses Sierra and me. Then she goes to meet my father.

Sierra and I sit down at the kitchen table.

"Baby, I promise that I'll keep Vernon informed of my every move, and I'll have him help me when I make the bust. I will have backup from some of my friends, and Agent James will have my back. I'll be fine. It should only take me a few days to get in and out of the situation. I won't be taking a lot of time. I know Dad's situation. I won't forgive myself if something happens to him and I'm not here. I won't make you worry any more than you have to, baby. Please trust me on this, Sierra?" I gaze deep into her almond-brown eyes.

"Joe, I trust you. It's her I don't trust, but if that's what you feel you have to do, I'll be here praying for you to come home safe to me."

Sierra pulls me to her and kisses me more passionately than she has in a few days. I stand and pull her into my arms and fall into her embrace, trust, and love. A tear rolls down my cheek as I kiss my wife.

"Hey, there won't be anymore of this, sweetheart. I won't have you crying anymore, baby. I'll be careful. Thanks for believing in me."

"Just don't give me a reason not to trust you, okay?" Sierra says as she hits me in the arm and tries to smile. "I'm going upstairs to make sure the kids aren't terrorizing your dad."

"All right, I'm going to holla at my boy outside for a minute and try to see if we can get in contact with Mo-Mo and St. Louis Slim."

I go out onto the porch and my brothers are talking with Dino, my neighbor from across the street. Dino is like a little brother to me. I helped raise him and taught him to play football and basketball. He went on to be quite a basketball player at Hogan High School. Dino is almost as tall as my brother Paul, and about two shades lighter.

"What up, Catdaddy? What's up, fellas'? How's Pops doing?" Dino asks.

I shake Dino's hand, give him a hug.

"What up, dawg? Dad's hanging tough. What's been going on with you?"

"I've just been chillin', that's about it," Dino answers.

Aaron says, "Dino, I heard you been doing pretty good since you got that promotion at the plastic company, my brother."

Dino blushes. "Yeah, I'm a foreman now. I got an eight-dollar an hour raise. It came in handy, too, with the child support I gotta pay."

I remind him, "Dino, you know you getting paid. You only have one child."

"Don't be doing that monkey dance around here cause nobody's going to feel sorry for your ass today," John says as we all start to laugh.

"Damn, how you gonna be counting my money, dude. I'm doing all right, but my ex-girlfriend is trying to make me pay out the ass for my little girl. She gets joy from that shit, telling my friends that I'm paying for her new car and stuff like that." He clenches his teeth. "She makes me want to scream sometimes. Shoot, I feel like shouting now as a matter of fact."

I shake my head. "Whatever, dude. Stop whining like a punk. If you didn't want to pay, you didn't have to lay. That's my motto. The kid didn't ask to come into this world, so be a man and handle your business."

"Damn, man, I can't get no sympathy?" Dino throws his hands in the air.

I put my hand on his shoulder and look him in the eyes. "Dino, if you want sympathy, look behind 'shit' and 'suicide' in the dictionary." We all laugh.

But Dino just stares at us blankly, not seeing the humor. "Forget y'all, man. She's a blood sucker and I don't care what y'all say." He sits on the stairs.

"Aaron says, "Dino, we feel you, brother, but you can't focus on that kind of thing. If money is her master and she's doing you wrong, it will all come back on her, so don't trip. Put it in God's hands." Aaron gets up to go into the house.

Dino jumps up and shouts, "Dude, I believe in God and all, but He's not paying this child support. I am."

Aaron just shakes his head as he enters the house.

I push Dino in the head, "Boy you need Jesus!"

My other brothers leave the porch to enter the house as well, but not before they each push Dino playfully in the head.

Dino adjust his small neatly trimmed afro, puts his head down and smiles. His honey-brown skin on his face is reddened with embarrassment, "I know I do. That's why I go to church on Sundays. I'm trying. Honest, I am."

"Look, Dino, I need a favor, Bro. I need to get in contact with Mo-Mo and St. Louis Slim. I need their help on a case I'm working."

Dino, scratches his head with gives a smirk. "Joe, you sure you want to mess with them? They some dangerous cats and they run with a crowd that's out there, dude. I wouldn't even wish them cats on my baby's mama, man."

"Look, I know what I'm doing, bro. They owe me a few favors and now is the time I need to collect."

Dino walks around on the porch and rubbing his chin and back of his neck. "Man, you know that St. Louis Slim is still mad at you for breaking up that lip sync group y'all had," Dino says, frowning.

"I'll tell you what. Let me worry about St. Louis Slim, okay?"

Dino's bushy eyebrows raise and form a wrinkle on his forehead. He looks around to make sure we're alone. "You know them niggas' crazy, Joe. They into all kinds of shit. Them fools are more crazy than a crackhead on the first of the month."

"Like I said, crazy or not, them fools owe me, and I plan to collect. I can handle their foolishness and I can take care of myself."

"Well, I'll feel better if you take your partner Vernon with you when you go and see them. You know that St. Louis Slim like to play with knives and shit. He even pulled one on me once in an argument. He's fast with it, too. I didn't even know he had it, until he had it to my throat. I was going to kick his ass, too, but he had the knife and all, and we grew up together; so I let him slide," Dino says as he adjusts his shirt in his pants.

I roll my eyes. "Yeah right, Dino."

Dino playfully pushes me in the shoulder. "I guess I got to jack somebody up to prove to you that I don't play. Man, you just don't know who you be doubting." Dino puts up his fists to play box.

I push his hands away and put him in a headlock. "Dude, I ain't got time to be playing. Just give me the numbers."

"Let me go, Joe. Why you be playing all the time? You gon' make me have to jack you up. Let me go!"

I release him and give him a little push to let him know who has the upper hand. Dino frowns at me, and then writes down the numbers. "They both up in Topeka, Kansas. They're in the south part and always have some roughneck friends hanging around them. I have to admit, they have some very good-looking ladies, too. Good luck, dude, and remember what I said about Vernon going with you."

I shake Dino's hand. "Thanks, dawg, I'll keep that in mind. I'll call you when I get back. I'm going inside to tell my dad I'm about to leave. You comin'?"

"Yeah, I've been trying to get over here to see your dad. I've been helping your mom with a few things in the yard," Dino answers as he walks with me into the house and greets everyone.

Upstairs Sierra, Nia, the twins, and mom are around Dad's bed.

"Hey, everybody! Hi, Mr. Johnson, I just wanted to tell you I hope you start feeling better, and you've always been like a second father to me. I remember you whipped me once when you caught me in the store stealing candy. I thank you for that, and I don't eat candy to this day. I respect you a lot, Sir. I pray you peace and good health."

I put my arm around Dino's shoulders as he starts to break down and cry as he shakes Dad's hand.

"Dino, you a good boy and grew up to be a fine man. Always remember that, son," Dad responds.

"Dad, I'm about to leave, but I'll be back. You take care and you know I love you, right?"

"Joe, you know I know that. Take care, son, and come back in one piece. I'm not going anywhere until you get back, so take care of your business, and get that woman back here safe now, you hear?"

I grab my father's hand and with my other wipe the tear from my eye. "Yes, sir!"

six

IN CHASE'S ROOM AT THE HOTEL, SHE CAN'T STOP THE FLOW of tears from streaming down her face. She falls upon the bed, kicks off her shoes, and holds the pillows next to her.

"What is Agent James doing to help me out of this situation?"

Joe is on his way, but with them moving around so much, finding her will be very difficult.

They return to Nebraska in the morning and hopefully there won't be anymore surprise adventures like tonight. She turns on her back. Rain taps the window and tiny droplets roll down the windowpane as the lightning lights up the sky. The thunder booms from far off, but it's getting closer each time. A knock comes at the door, and before she can answer, Dread walks in and sits next to her on the bed. The rancid scent of cigar fills his clothes.

"Why do you cry in the dark, my dear? You have everything. I make you happy, no?"

Chase wants to run and hide, but is too tired to move. She decides to play along, but won't give in to any sexual advances from him.

"Dread, I'm just tired of all the killing and drama from earlier this evening. I'm also not happy with the way my fight ended in Nebraska. I'm sure you understand."

"Don't be foolish, love. I have to do dat'. It's only business. I do like dat' honesty about you though, Chase," he says as he squeezes her ass.

She grabs his hand and removes it from her backside. "Dread, I have to tell you that groping really gets on my nerves. I'm not a football. You need to learn something about being romantic. I realize especially after today that you take what you want, but I'm not one of those things. I give my body to whom I choose to." She sits up and moves away from him.

Dread grabs her by the waist and pulls Chase closer to him. "Is dat' right? Well, people have been taking from me since I was a child of God. I thought dat I was pleasing you, Chase, but maybe I've been wrong. I've been very patient wit' you, woman, because I do care, but do not take dis' kindness for weakness, okay?"

She does not like the tone, nor his hand moving up her inner thigh. How to keep him talking to take his mind off her? This situation is going to get violent.

"Dread, what did you mean by people taking advantage of you since you were a child of God? You really don't seem like a person that would want to kill and hurt people. You do believe in God, don't you?"

A loud burst of thunder roars, the wind picks up, and rain pounds the glass windows of the hotel room. The dew mist of moisture invades the air and Dreads hand slips from my thigh. The force of the wind blows the curtains side to side, and as a streak of blue-green lightning explodes across the night sky, it reveals a disturbed frown upon Dread's handsome face.

He slowly gets up and walks to the window. His massive frame blocks the wind that grabs his black wavy hair and tosses it in the cool breeze. He almost looks majestic.

His body illuminates as the glow from the lightning outside flashes against his silhouette in the darkness. He turns and looks at me with a lost expression, as he seems to be stirring up past memories.

"Chase, I care about you enough to tell you dis'. I have never told anyone dis' but perhaps it will shed some light on me. My family is from Cuba and they are devout Catholics. I was an altar boy who helped da' priests at da church during da' service. We had a beautiful church right off da' coastline in Havana. It was made of clay and brick, but we had colored stained-glass windows and da' church was adorned with brass."

Dread walks toward the balcony. He pushes the curtains to the side and looks out the window as he continues. "There was a glass oval in da' ceiling so dat da' sun would shine on da' congregation and da' moon would shine in at night. It was so beautiful. We also had a huge wooden hand-carved crucifix at da' back of the altar. Jesus looked down with his arms outstretched for mankind. We were well off because my father was a cattle rancher, but our community was poor. We had status in da' church because we were good contributors."

Dread walks over to the bed and sits next to her as the storm rolls past and the rain calms to light showers. It is cool and Chase starts to relax from the day's stress.

Dread lies across the bed with his large hands across the back of his head, staring at the rain-kissed windows. He continues. "I would serve mass at da' church three times a week. I was nine years old and it was raining just like tonight. My father had to get home to help get da' herd of cattle, and da' Priest, Father Guevara Morales, promised to get me home safe. He said he needed help getting da' church in order after the service, so my mom and dad agreed. I liked Father Morales. He was a good man and always treated me special. Da' church community loved him, as did my family. He came to my home often for dinner."

Chase moves around on the bed fidgeting. Is he going to get to the point, soon?

"Dread, it's getting late and I've had a long day. Are we close to getting to the point?"

The wind has died down, but the rain is steadily pouring. The flashes of lightning are like a strobe light as Dread moves toward her. She throws her hands up. He stops in front on her and slicks back his hair. He takes a deep breath with his eyes closed, but his jawbone twitches.

"Chase, darling, can you stay up a few fucking seconds as I express to you my torment? I'm trying to be open to you. Do you not understand how hard dis' is for me?"

Chase composes herself and gives him her full attention, knowing very well that she just dodged a violent confrontation. She says a silent prayer that he continues.

"Father Morales asked me if I were hungry and I said dat I was. The ladies of da' church always made sure dat da' Priest had plenty to eat, so we walked to da' rectory where Father Morales resided. There was food a plenty and we ate til' we had our fill. There was chicken, beef, all kind of vegetables, and desserts. It was still raining very hard. It was hurricane seasun, but it was becoming dark very fast. I was kind of scared, so I asked Father Morales to take me home so I could be wit my family. He knelt next to me, placed his hand on my shoulder, and started to gently massage it. I pulled back."

A loud thunder boomed and they both were startled. Chase placed her hand on her chest to ease her rapid heartbeat. Dread went back to the window and settled against the frame, letting the mist of the storm gently spray his muscular body.

"Chase, I'm sorry dis is difficult for me. I have not spoken of dis and I'm not sure why I reveal it to you now, but I feel I must."

A child-like expression of innocence crosses his face as tears swell in his eyes. She sees a human side of Dread like he's reaching out to her. She's not sure if it's that he trusts her with such a hidden secret or that he really cares.

"Take your time, I'm not going anywhere." She's surprised that came out of her mouth.

"As I was saying, he was rubbing my shoulder and I asked to go home. He started to tell me how Priest was da' holiest thing next to God. He sensed dat there was an evil presence in me and asked did I know anything about exorcism? I told him no and he began to tell me how demons gets into da' body and only Priests trained in exorcism could expunge them demons out. I was a devout Catholic, so dis scared me. I asked him to help me and started crying. He said he would, but I had to trust him."

Dread shifts his weight in the window, like he is shifting the haunted memories in his mind.

"Father Morales walk me over to da' couch. He lit candles and turned off the lights. I think I was more scared of da' shadows dat were cast than the lightning, wind, and thunder from the storm. Father Morales came to me and pulled a small bottle of holy oil from his pocket. He starts to unbuckle my pants, but I pulled away. He says he was only going to bless me to keep the demons away. I still resisted, but he yanked my pants down to my knees along wit my underwear. I was confused. I asked him what he was doing and he said he was exorcising me. He gripped my neck wit his right hand as he unfastened his pants wit his left."

Dread wipes tears from his eyes. The pain he must have endured in holding all this in for so long.

He turns to her and continues. "He pinned me to da' armrest of da' couch wit his body as he poured the holy oil in his palm and rubbed it on his penis. He forced me to bend over and raped me. I was so ashamed and I knew dat he had to be the demon dat was inside me. I wondered why God would do dis to me. I served Him well and prayed to Him every night. I didn't deserve dat. Father Morales exorcised me several times da next couple of years."

Dread's hands are formed into clinched fists at his side.

"He would always make me take communion after his sexual exploitation. I would hold da' host under my tongue and would never swallow da' wine. He would try to force me to kiss him but I never would. He would even perform oral sex on me, but I just plotted my revenge. I went to da' Bishop and he slapped me. He told me to repent from such filthy lies and slander."

Dread crashed into the wall with his fist. Did he break his hand? He just stared out of the window.

"Father Morales was at our home so much da' dog even accepted him. The dog wouldn't even bark when da' Priest climbed into my bedroom window at night to rape me. My dad wondered what was wrong wit me when I nailed my bedroom windows shut. I told him that I feared the night and we left it at that. I think my dad might have suspected something, but was not sure. He never asked me out right.
After three years of da' attacks, I had enough and plotted my revenge."

A sinister grin spread over Dread's face.

"After Sunday service, once again I was at da' rectory. I had ground some glass and placed it in da' gravy that Father Morales poured into his potatoes unknowingly. I also crushed a cow tranquilizer pill and emptied it in his tea. When Father Morales had me in his room pinned to da' bed, he started coughing up blood. Da' glass had worked, cutting his insides. I broke loose from him and watched as he staggered and stumbled, asking me for help. I grabbed my baseball bat from under his bed and hit him as hard as I could in da' chest. He was short of breath and coughed up blood. I was not ready to kill him, yet. I wanted him to suffer like me."

Dread turns to Chase, a distorted, raged, sadistic look was in his eyes and face. It dissolved any sympathy. He walks closer to her and the damp night air caresses her as the chill bumps of cold and fear creep upon her skin.

"I kicked him in da' gut a few times and had him unbuckle his pants. I made him turn over and grabbed da' holy oil that he used on me, and let him watch me as I oiled the butt of the baseball bat. I hit his ass hard as I could in the back to keep him still, then forced da' butt of the bat into his ass as he'd forced himself into me. He screamed as I had, and it gave me joy. It was exhilarating. The more I forced the bat into him, the more he screamed."

Dread chuckles under his breath. "I finally had mercy on him and went to da' kitchen and grabbed a butcher's knife and bourbon whiskey. I came back up da' stairs and cut his throat, then poured da' fifth of whiskey on him and set his ass on fire. I wanted him to burn like he was in hell. I watched him squirm as da' fire consumed him. I smelled da' burning flesh, blood, and shit that spilled from his rectum, and it turned me on. I had never experienced an erection before. It was divine."

Dread sat next to Chase, putting his hand on her thigh. She was about to throw up. His eyes were ablaze in the darkness and he wore a smile.

"I went to da' garage and got da' gasoline for da' lawn mower. I burned da' rectory down wit him in it. I ran home and never told anyone what had happened. I believe da' Bishop suspected me, but who would question a child for something dat sinister? My cousin worked on da' police force in Cuba. He's da' one that helped me come over to dis' country and get settled wit some relatives here."

"So Dread, do you ever regret what you did to the Priest?" She asks.

Dread gives a half laugh. "Do you think dat' fuckin' Priest faggot gave a damn about me? He got what he deserved. I sent him in a fireball straight to hell."

Dread coolly gets up and walks away from me. He locks the door and saunters back slowly to the bed while unzipping his pants. Chase tries to run to get to her gun, but he grabs her and hits her in the head. She feels her clothes being snatched off as she blacks out from the powerful blow.

seven

I ADJUST THE VOLUME OF THE STEREO SYSTEM IN THE BLACK Corvette I picked up from FBI compound. It is equipped with two automatic short-handle rifles, a thirty odd six and a twelve gauge, a semi-automatic Smith & Wesson rapid fire .45, and a silver snub-nose Barretta .38 with infrared sight. All are in a fitted hidden compartment in the trunk. Speeding up the I-70 highway turnpike toward Topeka, I put in the Marcus Miller CD and turn it to "Amazing Grace."

"Man, this thing sure can move, but it feels like your ass is being dragged across the ground. It sits low to the ground, but it has a good ride," Vernon complains.

I turn down the volume and glance at him. "Vernon, thanks for coming along and understanding my position."

"Look Joe, I'm your partner. I still don't like this shit one bit. What you got yourself into, I'm not sure, but this stinks to the high heavens and I don't want to lose another partner. I contacted a couple of friends in the Federal Bureau to see if all this shit is legit. I can't believe you were going to try and leave me behind. You know I wasn't going for no shit like that. You always have to remember to keep an ace in the hole, and I'm your ace in the hole, my friend. What Agent James don't know, won't hurt his ass.

I still think something is fishy about this. Remember, you got that track-ing device in your ink pen, so don't leave it behind anywhere. Keep it with you at all times, so if we get separated I can find your punk ass, okay?"

"Yeah, Vernon, I will, partner."

Good thing I took Dino's advice and brought Vernon along. It made Sierra feel better about me taking the case.

"Thanks for having my back." I punch Vernon playfully in the arm.

"Look, Joe, I got a bad feeling about this. I'm still trying to get an angle on Agent James and why he would want you for this case. I just feel like we're being set up, dude," Vernon says as he puts a cigar in his mouth.

"Damn Vernon, we've worked with this guy for over five years. He hasn't given us <u>any</u> reason to doubt him."

"Yes, until now. My momma used to always say, A man that tells you where he buries his money ain't the fool. The fool is the one who tries to dig it up.' See, we never know why a person tells us something, but no one risks what they've worked all their lives for. It would have to serve their purpose."

I rub my eye brow and bite my bottom lip and let it mull over in my head. "Vernon, do you really think that someone as square and by the book as Agent James could be jacking me around? What's his motive?" I look at Vernon and he just bites down on his unlit cigar. "Vernon, dude, I think you're just tripping. You my dawg and all, but I just don't see it. He's got too much to lose."

Vernon takes the cigar out his mouth and shakes his head at me. "And how would you know what he has to lose and what he has to gain?" He puts the cigar back in his mouth and lets the window down in the corvette and stares out the window.

"Whatever, dude, you just plain tripping," I respond as I turn up the Marcus Miller CD.

I pull off Interstate 70 and pay the toll. Nightfall has greeted us as we reach the Eastside of Topeka and drive into the Ripley Housing Project off Fourth and Lake Street. The area looks dangerous as brothers hang on the corners as their jeans and khaki pants hang off their rear ends.

Children run under the streetlights playing, riding their bikes and foot scooters, but no adult supervision is visible. The houses are closely assembled like black folk don't need space. The fronts of the yards are scattered with broken bottles, crumbled potato chip bags, and beer cans. They lay there as gentle reminders of broken dreams and crumbled hopes, lying on unforgiving ground that doesn't ever give way to green grass, and dandelions.

The young men and women are in clusters of six to eight and scattered throughout the neighborhood and eye the corvette like we're Ed McMahon and the Publisher's Clearinghouse Team. Vernon quickly locks and loads his gun, and rolls up his window. I do the same, not sure what to expect from our seemingly social-deviant brethren.

We pull in front of 422 Locust Street, the duplex address Dino gave us for Mo-Mo and St. Louis Slim. The dilapidated duplex sits off the street, and about five dudes are in the yard and more start to gather around the car.

Vernon smiles as he looks at me. "I bet you're glad I came now, aren't you?"

"You know I am, partner." I load the gun in my ankle holster. "Watch my back, and follow my lead."

We get out and I hit the silent alarm on the car. We approach the house and it smells as if my boys are barbecuing. The gang of curious onlookers surrounds us.

"Damn, dawg, that sure is a nice car. Let me drive it around the block?" a big burly, gheri-curl wearing albino-skinned brother asks.

"Nah, dawg, I don't want that gheri-curl juice all over my leather seats. You can watch it for me though and I'll throw you out twenty when I get back, awwwrriiight?" I negotiate in my coolest homeboy voice. The group busts out laughing and starts jeering on the pigmentless brother.

"Damn, Yellowman, you gon' let him yank on you like dat'?" a skinny shit-brown, ashy-skinned teenager screams, showing his yellowing, buck-toothed smile.

The albino brother they call Yellowman starts to sway and swagger, then steps to me. Before he can bring his hands from his waist to his chest, I pull my snub-nose .38 from the holster against the small of my back and place the barrel of the pistol in the young man's flared nostril.

Vernon pulls both his guns and keeps the other homeboys at bay. He says, "All right, everybody take it easy and go back to kicking cans, playing who can gulp the forty ounce or whatever you homeboys do up here in Kansas, and let us do our business."

The crowd just looks at each other, shuffling.

I say, "Look people, we don't want any trouble. We're just here to visit our friends and eat some of that Topeka barbecue we smell cooking in the backyard. So we're just gonna have Yellowboy here walk us on up to the front door like the nice young man he is. We'll say hello to our friends, get some information, and be on our way. Then y'all can go back to terrorizing the neighborhood. Okay?" Smiling, I nod to Vernon.

I lead my obedient, new-found yellow friend toward the door. I pull my gun from his nose, wipe the barrel off on his T-shirt, and have him knock for us.

"Who is it?" a husky booming voice asks from behind the wood door.

The boy just stands there, so I slap Yellowman behind the head to respond.

"Yellow man!" he answers hesitantly.

The door swings open and a six feet-two, almost blue-black brother with silky skin stands in the doorway with a frame like he plays in the NBA. Bald headed, he has a slightly graying goatee. Standing shirtless reveals his rippled abs and a Glock pistol in his belt strap. It has always been his weapon of choice. He pulls the half-smoked cigarette from his thin lips and blows the smoke into the young man's face.

"Boy, didn't I tell you kids to stay the hell out my yard!" Mo-Mo yells, then looks at me curiously.

I say, "What up, Black man?"

Mo-Mo squints to make out the face he hasn't seen in ten years. "Joe Johnson, what the hell? Man, c'mon in. St. Louis Slim ain't gonna believe this shit," he says smiling as he ushers Vernon and me into the duplex and pushes Yellowman toward his friends. "Get out my yard, and y'all better not fuck with my friend's car or there's gonna be hell to pay. He's a Kansas City Detective and got a license to kick all y'all's ass, and when he gets through, it'll be my turn. Gon' get to steppin'."

The kids slowly disperse, mumbling profanities.

He closes the door and sticks his hand out to Vernon as we put our guns away. "The kids these days ain't got respect for shit. How you doing, friend? And you would be?" He grasps Vernon's hand and shakes it.

"Mo-Mo, this here is Vernon, my partner."

Vernon smiles at him and they shake hands and embrace. I can tell Vernon likes him by the expression and slight smile on his face.

"Nice to meet you, Mr. Mo-Mo. I like the way you handle them kids." Vernon laughs. "So, Mo-Mo stands for?"

Mo-Mo flashes his gold-tooth smile. "Damn, Joe. You slippin', dude. You ain't told the man about me. Well Vernon, I was MVP of the Kansas City, Central Blue Eagles 1960 Missouri basketball and football teams. My friends started calling me Mo-Mo 'cause I gets Mo of what the average man gets or wants and more; and the ladies think I'm Mo-licious, because I Mo-Mo-rize them."

Vernon smiles and shakes his head.

My friend's not lying 'cause women would just throw themselves at the fool and he took everything they gave and more. He had it like that and he knew it.

"Well, it's nice to meet you, brother," Vernon says.

"Man, y'all have a seat and rest yourselves. Let me get y'all a beer. I got some pimp steak on the grill, and if I say so myself, it's off the hook, man."

Mo-Mo walks to the kitchen as Vernon and I take a seat in the spacious living room. The inside is well-kept, clean, and neat. They have moderate taste in furniture and a picture of our old lip-sync group, The Time Revue hangs on the wall. I get Vernon's attention and show him the picture as Mo-Mo comes in with three cans of Colt .45 Malt Liquor Beer and three pimp steak sandwiches.

"Here we go. Here's just a little something to feed your soul and wet your whistle," Mo-Mo states as he hands us the cold beer and sandwiches.

Vernon looks at the beer before he opens it, sniffs its contents, and frowns. I can tell he got something to say. Then he smells and takes the bread off the sandwich and looks at the meat. "Damn, Mo-Mo, I thought you said you gets Mo than the average man. You gonna get Mo drunk drinking this malt liquor. This shit will kill you, brotha. I'm real thirsty and I don't want you to think I'm not grateful, 'cause I am. But a beer says a lot about a man and this looks like barbecued bologna, dude."

Mo-Mo looks at the beer can, takes a huge bite of his pimp steak sandwich, and then gazes at Vernon. "I just like it, man. Pimp steak is the bologna roll barbecued on the grill. It's a poor man's steak and a delicacy in Indianapolis where my old lady was from. Shit, I tried it and got hooked, brotha. It's Mo better than a fried bologna sandwich. It got a lot of kick to it, just like the beer, my man," Mo-Mo explains after taking a long sip.

"Yeah, maybe that's why they got that big-ass horse on the front of the can," I state laughing. "It got kick for sure. Remember man, we driving. We can't have this beer kicking our asses and getting us killed. The pimp steak tastes good though." I state laughing.

"Whatever, dude. This is some good shit," Mo-Mo brags.

Vernon holds up the can like he's doing a commercial. "Yeah, you can say that again. The shit part must come with the horse piss aftertaste."

Mo-Mo just waves us off as he picks up the picture. "Man, these were the days. Y'all had it going on. Shit, we all got some after these dudes would do their act. I just stood by and got the overflow chicks. Joe, you know your boy still mad about y'all breaking up the group." He tries his best to hold a stern look and we both burst out laughing.

"What's so funny?" St. Louis Slim asks from the doorway of his bedroom in red paisley, silk boxer shorts, slippers, a matching robe, and scarf that's wrapped around the back of his hair and tied in a knot in the front. He is of high-yellow complexion, stands about six feet, his hair is long, processed, and he is the splitting image of Morris Day of the black rock group, The Time.

"Sweet St. Louis, I see you haven't grown out of your childhood fantasy of going solo," I tease. "Vernon this is St. Louis Slim. Slim, this is my partner and best friend, Detective Vernon Brown."

Vernon goes over and shakes hands with my pretty friend.

"Nice to meet you, brother. Chili sauce!" Vernon says as he side steps as the group, The Time, dances in their song, "The Bird."

"Oh, I can tell you're one of Joe's friends, cause you ain't funny either. Ha-haa!"

St. Louis Slim laughs in his best Morris Day impression. Vernon falls on the floor laughing as I buckle over in laughter as well. I look up smiling as Mo-Mo rolls his eyes.

I give him a reality check. "Dude, I can't believe you are still caught up in that Morris Day bit. Man, we have been done with that for over fifteen years. You played a good part, but that's over. Get a life!"

"Joe, you're one to talk? You broke up the group, asshole. You were just jealous, because I had the lead and I was getting all the women. You should know, ain't nobody bad like me," St. Louis Slim says as he does a 360 degree turn and comes to a dramatic stop with his hands in the air and has an arrogant smirk on his face.

I walk up to Sweet St. Louis and get in his face. "Look dude, I created the group just for fun. For the sake of imagination, I created you. I got your wardrobe for you, taught you how to walk, dance, and act like Morris Day. I definitely had my share of women, because I was the brains behind the group, and the creative genius. All we did was have fun and lip sync, so stop tripping. It was all make believe, and you were the fool that ended it. Remember, going solo?" I start to laugh.

"Well, I was the star of the show. You couldn't have the group without me," St. Louis Slim retorts.

"And you couldn't go solo without a band, asshole!" I respond.

"Fuck you, Johnson. Why you here anyway?" St. Louis questions, visibly upset, and turns redder by the minute.

I look at Mo-Mo and back to Slim. "Fellas, I've come to collect on my favors. I need some guns and some back up. I know you guys got connections. I'm taking this case that will take me to a few different cities. I can't trust their local authorities, because they might be dirty."

Mo-Mo's face lights up and he smiles at me. "Joe, you got my support. We got some serious Glocks downstairs and a couple more surprises."

"Oh, so you just waltz on up here to Topeka and just think all's forgiven, huh, Johnson? Well, this sounds dangerous to me. Sounds like some folk can get killed real easy? What's in it for us?" St. Louis Slim asks. He takes off his scarf, flings it over his shoulder, and checks his hair out in the mirror, traces his thin eye brows and thick mustache with his index finger. He turns and faces me. "Damn, I look good!"

"Whatever, dude!' I say. "I can give you guys twenty thousand now and ten thousand when we finish the case. That should hold you over for awhile."

Vernon walks over to St. Louis Slim. "Brother, if I may, I've heard about you from some of Joe's friends on the block, and I've seen some pictures of the group around town. Would that have happened if Joe wouldn't have given you the chance? Look, I don't know what's between you guys, but Joe needs you on this one. He's going into this case blind and don't know who or what he can count on. I thought that at least he would be able to count on his friends, especially as much as he brags on y'all. We're trying to save the life of an FBI Agent and Joe needs to end this case as quickly as possible, because his dad is dying."

Mo-Mo comes over and embraces me. "I'm sorry to hear about Pops Johnson. You know your dad has been very good to St. Louis and me. We gonna help you out, Johnson. Ain't that right, Sweet St. Louis Slim?"

St. Louis nods and puts his head down as he walks over to me. "Why didn't you tell me about Pops, dude? Yeah, we got your back, Joe. We'll help you out. I got to make a few calls. C'mon, let's check out what you need in our munitions room, and you can fill us in on the details. I'm gonna let the group-thing slide for now, but we ain't through, Mr. Johnson." Sweet St. Louis turns on his heels and heads downstairs.

I roll my eyes and try to remember I'm grateful for his help. I hope I don't regret it, knowing that he's going to hold this over my head for a long time.

We grab our malt liquor beer, follow Sweet St. Louis Slim through the house and down a flight of stairs to the basement.

Vernon turns when we get to the bottom of the stairs and asks, "Why they call you Sweet St. Louis Slim?"

St. Louis stops in his tracks and throws out his robe for effect, as it slowly flows back to his side. He pulls out a big-toothed comb from the inside pocket of his robe and unhurriedly runs it through his permed hair. He bats his eyes at Vernon and puckers his lips. "Well, if you must know, my good man, that's the place of my origin. Yes, I was a cool little nip, gettin' wit' all the pretty young thangs with the big hips, wearing my Stacy Adam wing-tips, making sure my shirts and baggies were starched with creases as firm as a young girls tit's, I eat honey-glazed barbecue ribs tips and I love when they play jazz, like Georgy Porgy by the St. Louis Arch, watching river ships. Um-hmm, but gigolos get lonely, too. So, I moved up here with my boy and you know what? Our business grew. Ha-haa!"

St. Louis crosses his legs and does a quick 360 in front of the entrance, and pulls out a key that he places in the door. Vernon, Mo-Mo, and I all roll our eyes. My Morris Day look-a-like friend opens the door to what looks like a janitor's closet.

Good Lord! The state-of-the-art computer room opens into another space that has assorted guns, rifles, and automatic weapons encased in glass. A metal table in the middle of the room has a computer monitor and a hologram projector that has a map locator suspended from the center in laser matrix. St. Louis Slim and Mo-Mo grin and smile, like two proud parents.

Vernon takes out a cigar and places it in his mouth.

"Don't light that!" Mo-Mo and St. Louis Slim scream in unison.

"We got explosives in here," St. Louis states more calmly.

"He never lights it, he just like to chew on it," I explain.

St. Louis looks Vernon up and down, shaking his head. "Must be some Freudian thing. Ha-haa! Vernon got a little freak in him, don't you, Vernon? Yeah, Mr. Nasty man," St. Louis teases winking at him.

"Well, at least I don't dress like a freak," Vernon returns, pointing at St. Louis's red slippers and boxer outfit.

St. Louis runs his hands over his boxers, then looks at Vernon blushing. "Don't hate, dawg. You wish you looked this good!"

"Whatever; just show us what you got," Vernon responds, pushing past Sweet St. Louis.

Mo-Mo goes to Vernon's side and opens the glass case. He picks up the little balls that look like cherry bomb firecrackers.

"Be careful with those, Vernon. They make a big bang and can do some damage. It's filled with plastic explosives. That little ball can take out a metal door three inches thick. Take a few if you need them. They're activated twenty seconds after making initial contact. So throw them hard and run like hell or take cover," Mo-Mo explains as he places five in a small black case.

I peer at the semi-automatic machine guns. "Man, these are compact for machine guns. I probably can use one or two of these."

"These babies use snub-nose hollow-point .25 shell casings," Sweet St. Louis says. "You shoot somebody with one of them bullets and it's guaranteed to take them down. The bullet splatters upon contact. It can be messy, but you won't have many people standing when the smoke clears. Let me get you one. We got these babies on back order. I'm hooking you up, even though I'm short on stock, my man." St. Louis gives me the once over with an attitude.

He's probably still mad about the lip-sync group.

"Joe, try these night-vision goggles out," Mo-Mo says. "You never know when these babies'll come in handy. I'll throw in a couple of pair, they sent us five pair too many." Mo-Mo hands me the goggles that are as comfortable as sunglasses and fit like swimming gear.

Vernon tries on the goggles and takes the cigar out of his mouth. "Who's they?"

Mo-Mo and St. Louis Slim look at each other like Vernon has broken a cardinal sin.

Sweet St. Louis Slim sucks his teeth as he checks his perfectly manicured fingernails, "Hey brother, do I ask you what you and your wife do in the bedroom at night? Do I ask you who yo' daddy is? Do I ask you why you all up in our business like that?" St. Louis rolls his eyes at Vernon as he and Mo-Mo give each other a high five.

Vernon smacks his lips and frowns, "My bad dawg, but don't ever let my daddy's name come rolling off your lips again or I'll have to shove those red slippers up yo' narrow ass. You got that, Sweet St. Louie?" Vernon points his stubby finger at my friend.

Sweet St. Louis raises his eye brows with surprise, as he throws his hands up in the air. "Awe, hell naw! How you gonna come into my place disrespectin' me? My name is Sweet St. Louis Slim, not 'Louie', asshole. Don't let me have to slap the shit out of your old ass with these red slippers, okay?"

Mo-Mo holds Sweets back and I'm getting bored with the drama.

"Ain't nobody slapping nobody, today. Vernon, stop being so sensitive and Sweet St. Louis, stop being so cynical. Just show us what else you got so we can be on our way."

"Awe right, but your partna' better recognize," St. Louis says.

Vernon puts his cigar back in his mouth. "Yeah, whatever!"

My homeboy, turned-black-market-criminal friends, show us the rest of their goods and we pick out a duffle bag full of ammunition, explosive devices, and guns. We return to the metal table and I explain the case. We get a contact number and an agreement that they'll have my back when the time comes to get serious. They both agree and promise to contact Vernon if they hear of anything that will help in the case.

Vernon picks up the duffle bag and we prepare to leave.

"Uh Joe, what's up, dawg?" Mo-Mo asks, looking at St. Louis Slim as tho like he's missed something.

Vernon and I stop and turn around to face Mo-Mo.

"Yeah?" I ask.

"I think my friend wants to know how you two plan on paying for the merchandise you've just collected. This ain't no blue-light special at K-Mart, dawg. You got about sixty thousand in goods. How you gonna pay for that?" St. Louis questions rubbing his dark thin hands together.

"Well, let's see, I'm going to keep your asses out of jail by not busting up your little operation here, and turning you over to the FBI. I also have both you fools in my pocket for favors. You both owe me big time. Don't forget that, and this twenty thousand in cash should cover it. I'll need you guys in Nebraska tonight. I'm gonna need back up, and it's another twenty thousand in it for you when we get our friend, and the evidence to bust this Cattanno guy." I throw them a roll of thousand dollar bills.

Mo-Mo takes off the rubber band and fingers through the money and gives St. Louis a nod.

"We straight, brotha, and we'll be there tonight," Sweet St. Louis promises.

"Yeah, that's what I thought. Don't let me down, fellas. I'd hate to have to come back here on business," I say with a frown for effect.

"Joe, that evil stare shit didn't work when my mamma pulled it on me, so you know it ain't gonna work with you," St. Louis complains.

"Joe, you need to take that somewhere, brotha. You be trippin'. We ain't never let you down, so go 'head on," Mo-Mo assures me.

"Well, at least I tried it. You fellas hang loose and thanks for the love." Vernon and I shake my friends' hands and head for the car.

The car is like we left it and the kids stand on the corner where we first saw them.

"They good kids man, just need somethin' to do," Mo-Mo explains.

Vernon replies, "I can believe that, but surrounding people and trying to jack their car ain't my idea of something to do, if you know what I mean?"

I place the duffle bag in the trunk as St. Louis Slim comes out on the porch in his black/canary yellow pants and shirt outfit, accented with canary-yellow Stacy Adams shoes. He brushes off his sleeve and puckers his lips. "Ain't nobody bad as me!"

We shake Mo-Mo's hand again and get into the Corvette. Vernon rolls down his window and yells out as I pull away, "Get a life!"

Sweet St. Louis gives us the finger.

eight

THEY JUST FINISHED ROLL CALL AT THE NEBRASKA POLICE DEPARTMENT downtown precinct. Chase tries not to look at Dread, after what he did to her the other night. She went undercover to get next to him as a crooked cop. They started seeing each other. He has been aggressive and touchy now and then, but never tried to force himself on her sexually. Until now.

She always thought he was sexually dysfunctional. Shit, after what he did to her, he is sexually dysfunctional and payback is a bitch.

As the other officers slowly make their way out of the meeting room for morning roll call and duty assignments, she stands against the wall rubbing the handle of her police-issued .45 automatic. Cattanno made note of Officer Clark Malon's absence from roll call and has assigned a couple of officers to find out why he was not there. Of course, Brutus killed him after the snake bit him in the face, but it's all a façade.

Everything has its time and place, but this will be the last time that Dread or any of his men will place their hands on her in a violent way. She can't afford to blow her cover, but if she has to isolate them one by one and kill them, she will.

"Chase, you ready to put in some time on the streets?" Officer Brutus

Tucker asks as he approaches her with a small smile.

If Brutus didn't work for Cattanno, they probably could be good friends, but that slamming her into the ground incident has him on her hit list, too.

"Sure, Brutus, but let me run to the bathroom first," Chase replies as she heads down the hallway. She enters and makes sure no one is in the stalls, then pulls out her cell phone after locking the door and turn the faucet on full blast, so not to be overheard.

"Agent James, Chase here. We're back in Nebraska at Police Headquarters. If you send some men to Moville, Iowa, there is a field about three miles east from town. There you will find a Sioux City police officer burned to death in his squad car, and in the nearby field, six men that were massacred; all the work of Dread and his men. I need to get out of this. I can't take too much more and where the hell is my back up?"

"Agent Chase, you were trained for these situations. Keep your head and you'll get out of this. Detective Joe Johnson should get into town sometime tonight, I would think. He'll get in contact with you at some point when he thinks it's safe and won't jeopardize your cover. We found the body of Agent Smelley, like you said. We brought him here for an autopsy. His body is being flown to his family back to Nebraska later today. You make sure you make this case stick, Chase. I want this Dread son-of-a-bitch. I have the Governor here in my office and he assures me that we'll get all the resources we need to bring Dread Cattanno and his operations down."

This does not sit well with her. She never trusted the Governor since working on the investigation of the death of his daughter who was prostituting and abducted by the Missouri River Serial Killer. He had raped her before that, and she had a child from him. He also held up a search warrant they had asked for before storming the killer's trailer home. The guy is a major creep. What is his interest is in this case and why all of a sudden is Agent James dealing with him?

"What gives with the Governor? The last time I checked, he was way low on the creep sheet? Does Joe know that he's in on this case?"

"<u>You</u> wouldn't even be on this case if it wasn't for the Governor and his help in funding the expenses for us to get this dirty cop-killer off the streets. You know next year's an election year. He's the one that got us the money to send Joe in to get you. You should be kissing his ass at this point, Chase."

"You don't need to tell me who's ass I need to kiss. Right now, I'm trying to stay alive. I'm just wondering what's in it for him? There has to be a catch. Something just doesn't feel right about him being involved and how you guys got to be so chummy, that's all?"

"Chase, you just worry about staying alive and we'll worry about the rest after we get Cattanno behind bars in a federal prison. We need to find out who Cattanno reports to. Do we <u>have</u> that information yet?"

"Not at this point. He has never mentioned anyone he reports to and no one has come to the house. I would know that."

"Have you had a chance to look at his accounts or books of any financial transactions?"

Chase sighs, "Agent James, there are at least five people in the house on any given day, twenty-four hours a day. He keeps his records in the safe in his study. If I ever get the opportunity, I'll sneak in and take a look. I know the combination, though. I've watched him on several occasions. I just need to get in there unnoticed."

"We'll need some concrete evidence on this guy, Chase. We have to link him to the black ring. We need names of all the officers in this black ring so we can get them in one sweep. We only got a few more days to tie this up. I have inside information that Dread plans to head back to Cuba. If he gets away before we nail him, a lot of heads are going to roll. We'll be forced to explain what happened to the taxpayer's money, and there's a hell of a lot of it that's gone out on this case. So do what you got to do to get that information."

"I'll do my best. I have to wait on the right opportunity. I can't risk blowing my cover by getting caught and ending up dead. You won't have a case if that happens."

"Your best is not good enough, Chase. We need that information. You're the key to this case. Do what we sent you in to do. Detective Johnson should be in contact with you by tomorrow. I'll have him check in at the Marriott Hotel in downtown Omaha, Nebraska. You can contact him there. He'll be under my name, so you'll be able to reach him in his room by tomorrow afternoon. Be careful."

A loud knock comes on the door and someone is checking the knob. She quickly hangs up, turns it off, and returns it inside her panties. She quickly rushes to the toilet and flushes, goes to the faucet, wets her hands in the water and splashes her face, grabs some paper towels, and opens the door while drying her face and hands.

"It sure took you long enough. What you do? Fall in?" Brutus asks as he pushes pass her and looks into the bathroom skeptically.

"I was taking care of business, if you must know. Since when you been so nosey?"

"Nobody likes a smart ass, Chase? What's with the attitude? I was simply saying it took you a long time that's all," Brutus explains with a sigh and shrugging his big shoulders.

She takes a deep breath and tries to regain her composure, ignoring his glare for understanding. She hopes Joe is on his way and hopefully he'll have some answers and help her wrap up this case. They walk out of the building and toward the squad car.

The morning air is brisk and the bright sun peeks through the clouds. She tries and concentrates on getting on with the day, but thoughts of killing Dread Cattanno continue to dance through her mind.

They get in the squad car and Brutus turns to her, "Dread's called a meeting. We're to meet at Denny's on 12th and Central in two hours, so we got a little time to kill. You want donuts? I'm buying," Brutus says with a slight smile.

"Why not? We don't have any calls to attend to at the moment."

At the Donut Hole we get donuts and coffee. Brutus reminds her of a child as he shyly eyes the assorted confections and points out the sprinkled ones. He orders six and a large cup of coffee. Chase gets a couple of frosted and a small grape juice. They have a seat by the window so they can have a clear view of who comes in, the car, and the street.

"Chase, can I ask you something?"

She partially pulls the lid off her grape juice and inserts the white and red straw and takes a sip to wash down a bite of glazed donut. "Sure, what is it?"

Brutus devours one of his sprinkled donuts in two bites and wipes the remnants from his wide mouth with the back of his hand as he reaches for another and does the same, to my amazement.

"This will be between you and me, right?" he says through a muffled mouthful of donuts.

"You know that's gross, right?" she says, smiling. "Yeah, it's cool, but that goes for both of us, right?"

He takes a few sips of his coffee. "You'll have to excuse me, I was really hungry," he says blushing.

"I'd hate to see you when you're starving," I say, laughing.

"Okay, you got jokes all of a sudden, huh?"

"Somethin' like that, yeah!" she says with a tough-girl smirk.

Brutus snuffs down two more donuts and washes it down with coffee.

"Chase, you're an intelligent woman. You are very beautiful and seem to have a lot going for you. Why you mixed up with Dread?"

She eyes Brutus. Is he wired or not? "I have a thing for him, I guess. He takes good care of me. He buys me nice things and he provides me with a beautiful house."

"Yes, but he does the same things for the dogs. What makes it different for you?" His eyes are deep and gazing like he's trying to see inside of her.

She looks back at him, trying as hard as she can to hide the hatred for Dread. She puts on her best poker face. "Unlike a dog, I choose when to stay and when to leave. I am not obedient by any means, and I do have a choice. And the last time I checked, Dread has you on a leash like a little bitch, jumping at his every beckon and call, so what makes you so different from me?"

Brutus stops chewing and then bursts into a thunderous laughter. "That was cute, Chase, and that's what I like about you. You have spunk. I'm using Dread the way you're using Dread. We're a lot alike, you and me. We do what it takes to get what we want. We don't get attached and move on when people outlive their usefulness."

Chase drinks more juice and doesn't say a word. Sometimes if you let a person talk long enough, they'll tell you where they are coming from. She runs her fingers through her hair and put her elbows on the back of her chair.

"So you got it all figured out, huh, Brutus?"

Brutus shoves the last of his donuts in his mouth and nods.

"So, you're saying that to say what? I'm sure at some juncture in this conversation you're going to make a point."

"You and I both know we're not getting out of this alive, unless Dread is taken out. I know who's pulling Dread's strings. He has a boss and I know who it is." Brutus winks at her as he wipes his mouth and sees if any interest shows on her face.

She feels she's being set up, and has no reason to trust Brutus at this point. She's suspected that Dread was not the brains behind this black ring, but can't afford to blow her cover.

"You know this is dangerous talk, right? You saw what Dread did to the last person that tried to cross him and he has this thing about loyalty. I think we should drop this conversation, while the ball still has air in it, if you know what I mean?"

Brutus smiles and takes his Harley-Davidson magazine out of his back pocket and opens it up, covering his face. "Okay, Chase, consider the conversation ended. Oh, by the way, we're supposed to meet a Kansas City Detective tonight and welcome him to Nebraska, but you didn't hear it from me." Brutus winks at her as panic rushes through her body.

Does he know that she's an agent? If so, how'd they find out and how can she warn Joe? She hopes he was smart enough to bring Vernon for backup. She can't see Vernon letting Joe come up here alone, as tight as they are. How'd they get the information on what hotel he'd be staying at, and what time he'll arrive? There's a serious leak in the police department and bureau. She's sure Dread's money and influence has something to do with it.

"Brutus, why are you telling me all this? If you got a point, make it!"

"There's something I want, and there's something you want. Just think about it. We need to get going to this meeting. I'll drive," Brutus says as he gets up and heads toward the squad car.

So many things go through her head. Brutus is up to something and she needs to figure out what his angle is fast before he ends up getting them both killed.

When she gets in the car and fastens her seat belt, Brutus looks over his dark sun glasses, "Not a word of this to Dread, Chase."

She stares at him and let the moment's silence speak for her. As they roll through the Omaha, they don't say a word. The uncertain silence has her stomach churning as nervous energy flows through the police vehicle.

"How to warn, Joe?

nine

WE ARE ABOUT FORTY MINUTES FROM DOWNTOWN OMAHA, when I get this melancholy feeling that something is not right with my dad. I jerk over to the shoulder as dusk falls on the open road. I grab my cell phone and hit the speed dial to my parent's home.

"Joe, what the hell is going on?" Vernon groggily asks as he awakes from his slumber.

"I got to call my dad. Something doesn't feel right."

Vernon takes out a cigar, unwraps it, and places it in his mouth. On the fourth ring Mom answers, and I can tell by the gloom in her voice that she's been crying.

"Mom, this is Joe. How's Dad doing? Are you okay?"

Mom tries to hide her emotion, but doesn't do a good job. "Your father is slipping away from me, Joe. Sometimes he doesn't even recognize me. The people from Hospice came by at the doctor's request. They've been very helpful and are helping me cope with this. Your father's systems are slowly shutting down. They say he only has about six days to live. Where are you, Joe? Why are you not here?" Mom starts to break down.

I let the car seat back and wipe the tears from my eyes. "Mom, I'm so sorry I'm on this case. I'll get home as soon as I can. Is Dad in any pain?"

"They're giving him morphine shots, so he's pretty comfortable. Sierra and the kids have been a Godsend, Joe. She's here now. You want to talk to her?"

"Yes, please put her on the phone. And Mom?"

"Yes, son."

"You know I love you, right?"

"I know you do and I love you, too. You be safe and watch your back, you hear?"

"I will, Mother. I'll be home soon."

Sierra gets on the phone and I melt when I hear her voice.

"Joe, I wish you were here. It's so hard seeing your father like this."

"Baby, I'm sorry I'm not there. Thank you for helping Mom. It really means a lot to me and my parents. Are things really bad?"

"Dad's a tough man, Joe. He has the kids around him when he's feeling well. He has them laughing and talks to them about Grandpa getting ready to go to Heaven, and that he'll be watching them from above. He told them when they do bad he's gonna come back and haunt them." Sierra giggles as both of us start to cry.

"Yeah, my dad is a character. I'll be home as soon as I can. Call me on my cell if he takes a turn for the worse. I'll be in touch, baby."

Vernon touches me on the shoulder as I wipe my tears and he takes the phone from me.

"Sierra, how you doing? Tell Gertrude that we're fine, and that we'll try and wrap this up as soon as we can. Tell the family I send my love, okay?" Vernon hangs up the phone. "Joe, you need to shake this stuff off, bro. I know it's hard, but we about to get into some dangerous shit. You have to have your wits about you and focus or we might as well head back to Kansas City and make funeral arrangements for Chase."

My father's never even been sick. I can imagine him in bed. I feel guilty as hell, but it makes me feel better that Sierra is there with the kids. I get out of the car, sit on the hood, and gaze at the golden and green sea of corn stalks that line the other side of the highway swaying to and fro like ocean waves.

"Vernon, this is harder than I thought it would be, but I'll get it together. We need to check in with Agent James to get our orders and point of contact." The sun slowly sets on the horizon, and I can't help but think if it's not symbolic of my father's precious life slowly fading from him.

Majestic orange, blue, yellow, and red encompass the sky line and birds fly away to some unknown place. The hollow breeze that blows across my face as a flock of geese flies over-head their wings falling up and down as if they wave good-bye to me. My father's presence surrounds me and I smile. Things will turn out for the best. I'll get back to his bedside in time for him to cross over. I promise myself that.

I dial the number to Agent Royal James' office and the FBI Headquarters in Kansas City. He answers on the second ring.

"Detective Johnson here. I'm outside Omaha. I just wanted to check in and find out who's my point of contact?" Since Agent James doesn't know that Vernon is with me, it's better to keep it that way; just in case my feelings about this situation turns out to be true, Vernon will be my trump card.

"Good to hear from you, Joe, I talked to Agent Chase earlier today and she's fine for now. Dread has struck again, though. We found six men that were shot in the back in a field in a nearby town. Seems like the poor bastards were gunned down, while running for their lives. There was also a Sioux City Police Officer killed and burned in his squad car."

"Was there any evidence fingering Dread Cattanno to the murders?"

"Yes, Agent Chase was an eye witness, but without her we don't have a case. We also need to get the list of dirty cops that Dread is connected with. I hear he keeps the list closely guarded in his study safe. One more thing..."

Amazing how much damage this guy has done and how Chase handled being in the middle of that mess.

"There's more?" I ask.

"Yes. Agent Smelly was hung up, beaten, and gutted. We found him in a barn there in Nebraska. His body has been released to his family. They were pretty torn up."

Anger swells inside me and I'm not sure it's because of how Smelley was killed or that it's being compounded by suppressed feelings about my dad. Whatever the case, my left hand clenches into a tight fist.

"I feel for their loss and Dread will pay. Where should I report and who is my contact there?"

"Joe, I've arranged for another agent, Epiphany Duvall, to meet you. She's from Dallas, and she's a bad-ass chick. She's been briefed on the case and she knows what you look like. She'll contact you at the hotel. She'll fly in tomorrow morning. Your room will be under my name. Everything has been taken care of, so don't worry about anything. Just show your identification. You'll have a suite at the Downtown Marriott. We also have an inside man at the hotel, Agent Jason Phillips. We call him, 'Little Tiny.' You'll know why when you meet him." Agent James chuckles.

"You know how I feel about working with people I don't know. So how am I approaching this Dread Cattanno when I get into Nebraska?"

"That's why I got you the best agents to back you up. Don't worry about Dread, he'll contact you. Word is out that a bad-ass Detective from Kansas City is out to get with his group. So I'm sure he'll have something up his sleeve to test you, so be careful."

"I'll do my best. I'll contact you when we have the list of rogue cops."

I hang up and fill Vernon in on what's about to happen as we get back in the car and continue our drive.

"So, does he know I'm with you?"

"No, Vernon, and let's keep it that way."

"Do you think that Sweet St. Louis and Mo-Mo will get in tonight?"

"I'm sure they will. They haven't let me down to this point. We're supposed to be matched up with two FBI agents, Epiphany Duvall and Jason Phillips. They call him, Little Tiny."

"Awe hell no, Joe. You know how I feel about working with people I don't know. Shit, they can get you killed. I'm already having doubts about your two friends from Topeka. Them boys don't seem to be wrapped too tight," Vernon says as he looks in the side-view mirror.

"Relax Vernon, it's already done. Mo-Mo and Sweet St. Louis know what to do, and they can take very good care of themselves."

Vernon looks at me with a smirk. "Whatever!"

We drive through the city as dusk breaks into night and pull into the parking lot of the Marriott hotel. Before we get inside, Vernon grabs me by the shoulder.

"Dude, I forgot those pimp-steak sandwiches in the car."

I frown at Vernon as the young desk clerk listens on to our conversation wearing a plastic smile.

"Man, I thought you didn't like those pimp steak sandwiches."

Vernon shrugs his shoulders at me like he doesn't care either way. "Well, either I can leave them in your little sports car all night long and have it smelling like barbeque sauce in the morning, or I can go get them out, so we can have something to eat while I'm whipping your ass in dominos," Vernon says with a smile.

I turn to the cinnamon-brown-complexioned desk clerk with blond hair and a cute round face. She is so far into our conversation that her elbows are resting comfortably on the front counter.

I read her name tag, show her my FBI badge, and identification.

"Ms. Val Wilson, could you please tell me what room we'll be in? The room should be under the name of Royal James."

She smiles as she reddens. I smile back at her.

"Yes Sir, let me check the computer registry. Yes, here it is. We have you in the Presidential Suite. The sofa in the living area folds out into a bed or I can put you in a smaller suite that has two beds in it."

"That won't be necessary, the Presidential Suite is fine," I respond. I turn to Vernon.

"Whoever wins the best three-out-of-five games of dominos gets the bed, old man."

Vernon just smiles and winks at me as I turn attention back to Ms.

Wilson. "What's the suite number?"

"1812 and you'll need to insert your room key in the elevator to get to the eighteenth floor. There's a courtesy room on the twenty-first floor where you are welcome to complimentary cocktails, desserts, and appetizers. It will be open until 7 this evening." She hands each of us a plastic key card.

She asks batting her eye lashes, "Will there be anything else?"

"No thanks, Ms. Wilson, you've been most helpful," Vernon responds, pushing me in the back of the head.

"I'll meet you in the suite, and I'll bring the luggage up with me.

Vernon takes the car keys off the counter. "I might go around the block and find some juice or sodas to wash down them sandwiches," he says as he jiggles the keys in front of my face.

I start laughing as I grab the bags off the floor. "That's cool, bro; just don't be trying to catch no young ladies in my ride, fool. I don't want Gertrude having to whip your ass for trying to live a second childhood."

Vernon gives me a dirty look. "Why you always hatin', Joe? You're worse than that pimp friend of yours, Pretty Kevin. Always talking shit and can't back up nothin'. I'll see your punk ass in a minute," Vernon says as he walks toward the exit.

"Awe Vernon, man, don't be so damn sensitive. I don't hate, brother. Have a good time.

"Whatever!" Vernon states as he gives me the finger and leaves.

A huge bellman approaches. "Need some help with those bags, Sir?"

I look at the biggest bellman I've ever seen in my life. The guy stands six foot-two and looks to weigh about three hundred pounds.

"I think I can handle it, partner. It's only a couple of bags."

The overweight bellman grabs the bags, startling me with his persistence.

"I insist, let a dude do his job, Sir. It's been slow tonight and you never know when you might need your hands free, if you know what I mean?" He nudges me in the arm with his elbow.

Oh shit, Little Tiny. I give in to his persistence and enter the elevator. He motions for the suite key and I give it to him. He inserts it into the card slot in the elevator.

"What floor?" He grunts between breaths.

"The eighteenth. You all right, dude?"

"Yeah, I'm cool," he pats his bulging belly. "I've been working out earlier and I'm waiting on them energy bars to kick in."

We both laugh. He reaches out to shake my hand and introduces himself. "I'm Agent Jason Phillips; my friends call me, Little Tiny."

Puzzled, I ask, "Okay, I give up. Why they call you Little Tiny?"

He looks at me blushing, his pearly-white teeth spread across his smile, amused like he's holding back laughter. "Cause', ain't shit on me small, so they have to say it twice!" We both start to laugh.

He wipes his eyes from the tears of laughter.

"Seriously, Agent James sent me in to help get Agent Chase from undercover and to assist you in this task. You don't know it, but you have company in your suite. Our objective is to gather information. Joe, that means you can't kill anyone and we're to let these guys get away. Agent James told me how people have a tendency to come up dead around you."

"Oh, did he mention that I wasn't the first one to fire a shot?"

Little Tiny shakes his head and his jowls flop back and forth. "Naw, he didn't mention that. Just remember, I'm on your side and I don't want to come up dead, all right? There are five of Cattanno's men in the suite. I'll take two, and you get the other three."

I scratch my head and do the math.

"Damn, Little Tiny. You big as shit, and all you can take are two?"

He winks at me. "I told you I just got done working out, dawg. Work wit me. If I see you getting your ass kicked, I'll pick up your slack. Damn."

As we walk down the corridor and get closer to suite 1812's door, Little Tiny cracks his knuckles and I stretch my neck from side to side.

He whispers, "You ready, dawg? Remember, don't kill nobody and especially me."

"What if they're trying to kill us?" I whisper back.

"They're just sent to scare you and see what you're made of. Ain't nobody gonna need a body bag tonight. You just remember you got three and I got two. Just remember that, dawg."

"Man, just open the damn door and let's get this shit over with, cause you're starting to get on my nerve with this I-got-two shit."

"Man, don't be getting all sentimental and shit on me. Calm your ass down. We on the same team. Agent James said you were all touchy and stuff."

"You and Agent James can kiss my ass. Just open the door, fool."

"Why I got to be a fool though, dawg?" Little Tiny complains as he inserts the key in the door and opens it.

We each grab a bag and enter the dark room. I switch on the hallway light, and just as Little Tiny said, the men were in different parts of the suite. One is at the bar drinking out of a miniature bottle of scotch, two stand in the living room, another is seated on the couch, and one walks out of the bathroom zipping up his pants. Little Tiny and I are quickly surrounded.

My mind is moving fast and I think to try and buy some time, until Vernon shows up to even the odds a little. I'm also hoping Mo-Mo and Sweet St. Louis will get here before anything gets physical.

"Oh, excuse us, we must have the wrong room," I state, but me and my FBI friend are quickly accosted from both sides.

The biggest of the men, probably the leader, walks up to me. He is a muscular white guy and looks quite menacing. "Detective Johnson, why are you here?"

I try and remain calm and cool, sizing up this man in case I have to take him down.

"How do you know my name and who are you?"

Before I can get another word out my interrogator slaps me across the face hard. I'm starting to get pissed. I look at him with a serious gaze.

"Hey, there's no need for that." Little Tiny says. "Let's just all be cool. I can get some free sandwiches on the house and have them sent up, and I'm sure we can work this room mix-up out like gentleman."

He is quickly punched in the stomach, which doubles him over.

"Dude, I just worked out. Why you trippin'? Damn, that hurt."

"You fools need to start answering some questions," the big white guy says.

"I'm here to hook up with some guy named, Orlando Dread Cattanno. I heard he has a way of making a cop some extra money. I love money and nice things, so I thought I'd come down and make his acquaintance."

"Well, we heard you've come to take Dread down and that shit ain't likely to happen," the muscle-bound man states as he takes brass knuckles out of his pocket and places it on his hand.

Little Tiny and I look at each other, neither one of us expecting this.

"Awe hell naw, what you need them for? Dude, I don't even know this cat. I was just bringing up his luggage. Man, y'all don't even have to tip me or nothing. I got a very short memory, and this ain't none of my business anyway," Little Tiny whines, looking at me and winking, then giving a sorrowful gaze at his assailant for mercy.

"Shut up, fool!" he barks at Little Tiny.

He turns his attention to me and my patience is getting very thin.

"Detective, you got one more chance to answer my question or I'm going to turn your face into hamburger," the big guy demands.

His lynch-men hold onto me and my FBI friend with our hands held behind our backs.

"Look, dude, I don't want nobody to get hurt. I'm just looking to score a little cash on the down low and be on my way. You don't need to be punching people around. We know you a bad ass and all that. I have to tell you, if you hit me with them brass knuckles, I'm going to kick the shit out of you and you can believe that."

The big guy bursts out laughing and all his men fall in doing the same. I just look at him, then at Little Tiny to let him know I'm not about to let this go too much further.

Little Tiny squirms from under the goons holding him, like he's trying to get to me. "Man, why you have to say that shit. You starting trouble, man."

"That's the first smart thing you've said all day, fat man," the big guy states.

Little Tiny's face contorts like he just tasted something sour and he stares at the rude man, showing that he didn't appreciate that last remark.

"Dude, I don't like being called fat. I'm working out, okay. Why you got to try and put people down and shit?"

The big guy walks up to him and pushes his finger into Little Tiny's bulging belly. "Well, that work-out shit ain't working for your fat ass," he says.

Tiny lunges for him, but is restrained by the men holding him. Hit in the face with the brass knuckles, he falls to his knees in pain. His round face is quickly swelling and turning red from the blow.

I tense up. "Leave him alone, asshole!" I am hit across the jaw as well. My head rings and it feels like the right side of my face is burning. I kick one of the guys holding me on the outside of his knee, making his leg buckle beneath him. He falls in excruciating pain.

I head butt the other man holding me, breaking his nose. I elbow the big white guy in the face, after blocking one of his punches. He falls back as I lunge on top of him, not giving him time to react. I commence punching him in the face.

Little Tiny has pushed one of his aggressors into the wall and has the other man by the nuts when Vernon walks in eating pork skins.

"What the fuck?" He drops the pork skins and bags from the store and pulls his gun.

"Cease and dessist!" Vernon demands.

I get up and start kicking the shit out of the big white guy. "So, Mr. Brass knuckles, you like hitting people, huh asshole?" I stomp the guy in the ribs and shoulders.

"Joe, that's enough!" Vernon orders. "Y'all sit y'all's narrow asses down over there on that couch!"

I go to Little Tiny as Vernon collects the guns and identifications from our assailants. All of them are cops.

"You all right, big man?" I ask as Little Tiny's jaw is bulging.

"Yeah, I'm cool. Where them knuckles at?"

Vernon throws them to him. Tiny walks up to our interrogator and whips him one across the face. "I just wanted your ass to see how this shit felt. Where's the refrigerator? I need to put some ice on this shit." Tiny looks around the room as he holds his swollen jaw.

"Yeah, I heard that. Get me some, too," I say.

I go to the table and look at the men's identifications. The big guy that has smacked us around is Officer Rick 'Brutus' Tucker. The other men are Officers Ronnell Jenkins, Stanley Turner, Adam Fletcher, and Christopher Hunter.

"You guys are pathetic. An officer of the law is never to give up his badge or gun and I have both. What will your boss think of that?" I ask as all the men glance sideways agitated, except for Officer Brutus Tucker.

"Shit happens," he replies with a smirk.

"So Brutus, you need a little ice on that jaw, dawg?" I tease.

"Fuck you, asshole! I'll finish the job next time."

I slap him on the swollen side of his face and he grimaces.

"Oh, did that hurt? I think you need to learn a little respect, Mr. Man. So let me see if I can assess this situation. You're Cattanno's flunky, right? Probably his poor excuse for a right-hand man?" I put the ice to my face that Tiny has handed me.

"I slapped you pretty good, huh, punk?" Brutus asks smiling.

I back hand him across the face for good measure. "Yes you did, but not as good as I slapped your monkey ass. Now as I was saying, before I was rudely interrupted. Cattanno sent you here to find out if I was legit. Well, yes I am legit. I'm one bad mother fucker, and to prove it, I got all of you sitting here like little bitches. I got no beef with you guys, I'm just trying to score some extra cash. Y'all tell Cattanno that when you get back, and if he wants your badges and guns, he needs to come to me himself to get them. I got a feeling that he ain't gonna be too happy when he sees y'all. You can go."

"Hold up, Joe. At least shoot them in the ass, the foot, something. You gonna just let them waltz out of here?" Little Tiny asks pacing the floor and turning red from anger.

I push Tiny back as he rushes toward the men.

"Remember, you work and live here; I don't."

He realizes that I'm protecting his cover and he plays along.

"I was just playing, fellas. I hope y'all have a great day and come to my hotel anytime and drinks will be on me," Little Tiny says as he backs away.

Vernon gets up and opens the door to the suite and motions with his gun for them to exit. They file out one by one and Brutus stares at me as he exits. We close the door behind them.

"You know they gonna be back, right?" Vernon asks.

I shake my head having already thought of their options, "I don't think so. Cattanno will want to get those badges back, because they can't work without them. He'll want to meet."

"Detective Johnson," Little Tiny begins, "We'll be having another agent help us on this case and she'll be in contact with you in the morning. Her name is Epiphany Duvall. I heard she's all that, and then some. I'm heading back downstairs to keep watch for trouble. I'll call up if anything goes down. Man, y'all need to straighten up this room, dawg. House-keeping is gonna flip if they find this place tore up like this," Little Tiny says, shaking his head. He holds ice up against his jaw as he exits the room.

Vernon and I look at each other and start to tidy things up a bit.

"Shit, I thought that's what housekeepers got paid for. To straighten things up! Damn!" Vernon complains.

"Watch your mouth, Vernon. We might get some company and we don't want to look like we've trashed the place."

"Y'all did trash the place! What kind of shit is that?"

"Vernon, if you could start helping and stop belly aching, we could be done very quickly."

"Whatever, dude," Vernon says as he collects the guns and badges and places them in his briefcase, after unloading the guns.

I pick up our bags and place them in the bedroom. A knock comes at the door. We both pull our guns and stand on either side of the door, ready to fire.

"Who is it?" I ask.

"Jehovah's witnesses!" a high-pitched voice answers.

"Ice cream man!" another husky voice joins in.

"It's R. Kelly! You got any candy and little girls in there?" another asks.

"It's your wife's baby's daddy," another voice shouts as a thunderous roar of laughter explodes from the hallway.

"Open the damn door, fool!" someone shouts as they loudly knock again.

We pull open the door and there stands our ex-pimp friend, Pretty Kevin, along with Mo-Mo and Sweet St. Louis Slim. Vernon rolls his eyes, heads to the table, and pulls out the dominos.

"What up, fools? Y'all almost got shot! Y'all play too much!" But, I'm happy to see my friends.

We give each other some dap and hug as we greet.

Pretty Kevin stands there in his black Sean Jean sweat-suit, flawless ebony hued skin, wide-toothed grin, and fly hair cut. "Joe, it's good to see you and Vernon. We would have come in sooner, but we were listening to some old tapes of the only King of Comedy, Richard Pryor. You guys doing all right?"

"Where were you guys when we were getting our asses kicked?" Vernon asks as he puts his cigar in his mouth.

"We? I'm the one with the swollen jaw," I remind him.

"Well, hopefully that will keep your shit talking down," St. Louis Slim adds, laughing.

"I ought to slap you for wearing that lime-green suit in here, and where'd you find shoes to match?"

St. Louis Slim brushes his sleeves and checks for wrinkles. "Don't hate! Congratulate! And you know ain't nobody bad like me. Remember that, cause I make shit like this look oh, so very good," he states as he strolls over to the domino table and sits by Vernon.

"Joe, we been here at least twenty minutes," Pretty Kevin says. "Agent Chase called me and said you were in trouble and are in a bad situation. She said that you were headed this way. She was worried about you and thought you might want some help. I called my boys and they said you just left. So we met up, and now we're here to save the day. We got your back, dawg."

"Yeah, I can tell by all that laughter in the hallway. Did Chase say where she was?"

"Naw, but we got a very good idea where she is."

Mo-Mo walks up and puts his arm around my shoulders. "Joe, we were sitting out in the parking lot when these five guys came out arguing. They had bad news written all over them, so we got the license plate number and called in a favor to a police friend, who ran the plate and we got the address of a house. We asked the sister at the front desk and she said it was on the edge of town. It's a big-ass, expensive, fortress kind of a place with about four or five guards around the perimeter. How is that for having your back?" Mo-Mo asks as he goes to the refrigerator. "Man, all y'all got is soda and juice? Damn, man, I'm hungry. Can we eat these sandwiches?"

"Vernon and that damn juice. Didn't we talk about that shit, old man?" Pretty Kevin asks.

Vernon gets up and walks over to Pretty Kevin. "Ain't you got your ass whipped enough for calling me old?" They both laugh and hug. Pretty Kevin gives Vernon the address to the cop's destination.

"What you wanna do, Joe?" Vernon asks as we all sit around the table.

I rub my eye brow, bite my bottom lip, and look at all my friends. "Well, we can't just bust up in there and rush the place. I think we should chill. He'll call and then we can determine what needs to be done to get the information. We need to bust his ass and get Agent Chase out."

Sweet St. Louis Slim rubs his stomach, "Yo, I'm hungry! Can we eat these sandwiches or what?"

"Man, I ain't in the mood for no pimp-steak sandwiches, nigga. I didn't drive all this way to eat bologna," Pretty Kevin complains.

"Joe, we got the suite next door to you guys and we charged it to the FBI," St. Louis Slim says.

"How in the hell did y'all do that?" Vernon asks.

"Sweet St. Louis told the front clerk that we were working on a case with you guys. You know no woman can resist Sweet St. Louis Slim," Mo-Mo says in adoration.

Vernon, Pretty Kevin, and I just roll our eyes.

"Whatever, Mo-Mo. Where are your pom-pom's and Bobbi socks? Shit, you might as well do a cheer for your boy," I tease.

"Damn, Joe, Agent James owes me anyway for locking a brother up for nothing," Pretty Kevin says as his snaps his fingers. "Fuck that, brotha. We gonna order room service courtesy of the FBI. You can put them sandwiches back, dawg. We're living high on the hog tonight."

Vernon shakes his head, "Kevin, you were the lead suspect in the case we were working on, and remember, it was your hookers that were coming up dead. We had no choice, but to arrest you."

Pretty Kevin snaps his fingers again, "Fuck all that. I still ain't eating nobody's bologna, man. Not tonight. So y'all can put them pimp-steak sandwiches back in the refrigerator where they belong. We're ordering room service courtesy of the fucking FBI."

I finally give in, grab the phone, toss Mo-Mo the menu, and dial room service.

ten

DREAD AND CHASE ARE EATING DINNER IN SILENCE ACROSS FROM each other as Brutus, Ronnell, Weasel, Adam, and Christopher walk in through the kitchen with their plates and sit at the table.

"Wat's da' meaning of dis? Do we have news of da' Detective?" Dread asks as he wipes his mouth with his napkin.

He searches the faces of his loyal comrades, while pushing away from the table. They all look at each other. You can tell something has gone terribly wrong.

"We had a problem, boss," Brutus fidgets with his hands.

Weasel puts his head down and adds, "He had another guy with him. I think he was a bellman. He had to be around three hundred pounds, we lost the guns and badges."

Brutus says. "We just fucked up. We'll make it right."

Dread laughs, sits back in his chair, and tosses his napkin on the table. "So you mean to tell me dat' one cop and a fuckin' bellman took out my men? Pleaz' don't tell me dat'. Wat kind of fuckin' cops are you, anyway? Brutus, I hold you responsible. You have to make dis' right. You get those badges and guns back or I'll have to deal with you," Dread snarls as he tosses a switchblade at Brutus's head.

It barely misses, but sticks in the high-back oak chair where Brutus is sitting. Brutus swallows hard, but says nothing. He never takes his eyes off Dread.

"I won't miss next time," Dread promises. "I will call dis Detective and you guys will be waiting down the ridge. There you will drive dis fucker off da' road. That should shake his ass up. I do like his persistence. You fuckers don't eat from my table! Leave my sight, you pieces of shit!"

The men rush from the dining area. Brutus is the last to leave, and Dread grabs his arm as he walks by.

"I am very disappointed. You do understand my position, yes?"

Brutus looks at him, then at Chase. "I understand," he replies as he exits.

Dread walks to Brutus's chair and pulls the knife out of it. He takes out his cell phone and makes a call. "He's here. My men failed, but will deal with him in da' morning. I think I like dis guy. I am looking very forward to meeting him, if he isn't killed first." Dread laughs into the phone and hangs up.

"Who is he talking to?" Chase thinks to herself.

He walks up to her and strokes her hair. "I'm taking one of my cars out for a drive to calm my nerves. Have on something sexy when I return. I will need to work off some stress, and I don't want to have happen wat' happened da' other night. Be nice to me and I'll be nice to you, yes?"

Her skin crawls. But, nod. Dread kisses her on the cheek and leaves.

She goes to the window to watch him drive off in the brown Ferrari. She passes through the kitchen, and the five scorned officers are watching TV and eating. They're all too defeated to even look up at her. This is the perfect time to sneak into the study to get the information from the safe she needs. Chase only has to get past one guard inside the house.

She walks through the game room and past the library, and has yet to see Byron Moore, who has been assigned to guard the inside of the house. Dread has cut down the number of men used to guard the inside, placed them around the parameter of the property. She thinks he's getting paranoid after what happened in Sioux City, Iowa.

The toilet flushes, so she quickly enters the study and carefully closes and locks the door behind her. She takes the pen light that has been holding her hair up and turns it on, shining it on the Charles Bib signature painting that hides the safe.

As Chase starts to enter the combination, she hears someone checking the door. She quickly spins the combination on the safe, closes the picture, turns off the pen light, and tries to think of a reason for her being in the study.

When Byron comes through the door with his gun drawn, he turns on the light and she is on the leather couch.

"What are you doing in here, Ms. Chase?" he asks as his face turns red with embarrassment.

Chase lies on the couch with nothing on but her thong and her arms cover her breasts.

"I'm waiting on Dread if you must know, and if you know what's good for you, you better get out of here before he catches you. God knows what will happen. You know how jealous he is, Byron."

Byron drops his gaze, trying not to look at her as he apologizes and closes the door.

Chase relocks the door, runs back to the safe, and grabs her belt buckle with the built-in camera. Upon finally opening the safe, she finds Dread's address book. She photographs all his contact names and bank-account information. When she finishes, she places them back in the safe exactly as they were and smiles.

She redresses and steps into the hallway where Byron is waiting.

"I thought you were waiting on Dread."

"I was, but you spoiled the moment, asshole. I'll be in my room."

"Hey, I'm really sorry, and uh, you don't have to mention this to Dread, do you?" he asks playing with his shirt collar.

"Not this time, but don't let that shit happen again. And I saw you peeking at my breast, Byron. Did you get a good look, asshole?"

"Yes, Ma'am, I mean, no Ma'am. I really wasn't trying to look. I swear." He's perspiring.

Chase just stares at him and climbs the staircase to her bedroom.

Her hands are trembling. She goes into the bathroom and splashes water on her face. Her nerves are shot and she still has Dread to deal with. She starts to feel like a whore for the FBI. She looks at herself in the mirror and doesn't like what she sees. But, has the information that she was sent in to get. Now, if she can just get out alive.

She puts on a crotchless, sheer, black body suit, goes to the window, and looks out for Dread's return as she dials Agent James's cell phone number.

"Chase? Good. Have we got any more information?"

"Yes, I have all the information that we need. I'm ready to come in," she answers.

"Great job! I knew you could do it, Chase. Things have changed, though. It seems that there is someone who Dread is reporting to, and we need him as well. We need a name or something. Did any names stick out in the book?"

"Shit, I don't know; I was too busy trying to get the information without getting caught, so, I couldn't memorize all the fucking names."

"Agent, get a hold of yourself. I'm your superior, and you will answer me accordingly, understand?"

"You said all you needed was his list of names and contacts to close the case. You're not sacrificing your body for the Bureau, Sir. I didn't join to become a prostitute," she replies as tears swell up in my eyes.

"Agent Chase, I'm going to say this one time and one time only. You will do whatever it takes to get this case solved. Period! You joined the Bureau to get scum like Dread off the street. We all have to make sacrifices, Chase. I know it's hard sometimes, but that's what we do get next to people to expose them and take them down. Shit can't get personal; it's all part of the game."

"Well, it's a fucked-up game."

"Get me that information and we'll get you out. I promise. You're a great agent, Chase. There'll be a promotion after this is over. The magnitude of this case permeates that."

"Yeah, a promotion."

She hangs up feeling worse than she already did. As she sits in the window staring at the stars hopeless, she see a lightening bug caught in a spiders web and the spider descending upon it's prey and she can relate to the bug and it's torment as the spider approaches. Dread drives up the road and pulls into the garage. Agent James words circle in her head, "We all have to make sacrifices."

She turns off the lights, hides her cell phone, lights a couple of candles, turns on the CD player, and lets Billie Holiday sing her blues. What would Joe think of her, if he knew what was about to happen? She lies in bed and let the tears flow as she waits for Dread to come and violate her - all for the good of the FBI.

eleven

AT ABOUT 6 AM I WATCH THE WATER FILL THE BATHTUB. Vernon's snoring has kept me up most of the night, so I decide to spoil myself with a hot bath and relax before a busy day. I have a pretty good feeling that Dread will call some time this morning and want us to meet with him. That will probably be his trap to kill us. We'll have to survive the surprises he has in store. We need to win his trust with our resourcefulness, then take him down when he least expects it.

How is Dads health holding up? A sense of guilt stabs my gut. I should be there, but at this point, I can't turn back. Still I can't shake the shame of me being here in a hotel in Nebraska, while my father is home dying and suffering in pain.

I submerge myself in the steaming water and let it cover my face. Strange how sound intensifies under water, and if you listen, you can hear your heart beat as it pumps blood through your body.

I come from under the water, take a deep breath, let the heat enter the pores of my skin, and relax my mind. Sierra would be getting the kids ready for school: making breakfast; answering the twins' questions as they brush their teeth, and my little angel, Nia, being Mommy's assistant by helping the twins get dressed and put on their shoes. I smile as loneliness traces across my heart.

There is nothing more sensual than seeing my beautiful wife getting dressed in one of her business suits. I picture Sierra pulling her pants up over her silk stocking-covered legs, and her having me help her fasten on her necklace of choice. I had the privilege of zipping up her pants. That would always give me a chance to embrace her hips and rub her firm, full ass. I would always place a gentle kiss on her neck and hold her close to me from behind. I love the way she smells and the way she holds my arms, when I embrace her like that.

My thoughts are broken by a presence in the room. It's not my usual inner alarm that gets my reflexes on edge and makes me quickly reach for my gun that's sitting between the towels on the floor by the tub's base. I am calm, even though I'm sitting in the tub with my eyes closed, reminiscing. When I open them, I find a full-bodied woman, who has beautiful dark eyes.

Dark-skinned, dressed in a navy blue pants suit, she wears her hair in a short afro that accentuates her oval face. Her nails are perfectly manicured, and her full lips are painted red. With hands on hips, and she has a look of delight on her face - like a sugar-junkie child about to reach into a cookie jar.

"FBI Agent Epiphany Duvall, I presume?" I ask with no embarrassment.

"Yes, and you must be Detective 'On loan with the FBI' Johnson. You look almost as good as I thought you would." She shifts her weight and places her finger by her red mouth.

"Thanks, but if you don't mind…" I say as I start to get out of the bathtub.

"Oh no, don't mind me, sugar. You go right ahead and just act like I ain't even here. I like to watch." She blushes while leaning against the bathroom door way.

I hear Vernon moving around, and when he looks up and sees the woman in the doorway, he eyes me.

"What the hell is going on?" Vernon exclaims.

Before he can get the words fully out of his mouth, Agent Duval, with quickness and confident agility, pulls two silver-plated Smith & Wesson .45 automatic pistols from the back of her waistband. With arms crossed, she has one pointed at Vernon and the other at me. Vernon and I look at each other wide-eyed, impressed.

"Damn!" we say in unison.

"So, are you gonna shoot us, or are you gonna let me get dressed so I can explain this case to you?" I ask her.

Agent Epiphany Duval puts her guns away and throws me a hotel towel from the rack. "Now, you take your time getting out that tub, sugar, and we'll talk about a lap dance later, okay?" she says, winking. Then she turns to Vernon. "And look at you, Detective Brown! All this chocolate up in here! I like a man who wears Tazmanian Devil boxer shorts. You go, boy!" She slaps him on the rear. He retreats back to his room in total embarrassment.

I can't help but laugh as I get out of the tub. I wrap the soft, large towel around my waist and pull the lever to release the water from the tub. I grab another towel, and dry myself.

I say as I shake her hand, "So, Agent Duvall, I see you are very resourceful. We could have used you last night when Cattanno's men tried to rough us up."

She smirks at my remark. "Baby, Epiphany Duvall always gets here on time. Y'all must have took care of things, cause I see you are here standing in front of me. A little bruised, but still looking fine. I was able to make it here this morning, so here I am ready for duty. You need some help lotionin' up there, brotha? One thing I can't stand is an ashy man. Ohhh, that get's on my nerve!"

I grab the shea butter off the counter. "No, I think I can handle that by myself, and my wife gives me all the help I need, when I do have problems. But thank you for asking."

Agent Duvall licks her lips and sucks her teeth. "Don't start acting all uppity in here. I was just trying to help. Don't let me have to get ugly up in here."

We walk into the living area where Vernon joins us, now robed. "You're pretty good to be sneaking up on us like that. I like your style, and I'm glad we have someone professional on our side."

I look Agent Duvall up and down. Wow! I'm amazed at how she made it in the FBI with her weight being what it is.

"I know you brotha's are probably looking at me and wondering how a sexy black woman in all her fineness could possibly be in the FBI. All full-figured with plenty of me for someone to love? Well, let's just say, it's not what you got, but how you use it, honey!"

Vernon shakes his head and smiles. "You must use it very well. You a whole lot of woman, and I bet twice as smart. You were slick enough to get in here on Joe and me, and that's damn good. If you're good enough for the FBI, baby, you're good enough for me."

"Vernon, you're so sweet. Thank you for that, I think. Well, Vernon, I want to take you guys to breakfast, so I think you need to go in the bathroom and wash your ass. Let me know if you need some help, sweetie? Then I'm going to take you, Joe, Pretty Kevin, St. Louis Slim, Mo-Mo, and Little Tiny to breakfast. My treat," she says, winking at us.

Vernon's mouth and mine drop open simultaneously. Vernon states with his eye brows raised and blushing, "How in the hell…"

"Because, I'm just damn good," Agent Duvall, with her hands on her hips, says, "A woman always does her homework. A hundred dollars can buy a lot of information," she says laughing as she walks over and knocks hard on the fellas' suite door adjacent to ours.

"What!" someone yells.

"Get y'all's asses up! We're going to breakfast!"

The door swings open. My motley crew are all standing in their boxing shorts, wondering who this woman is holding two guns in their faces.

"Good morning, gentleman. Look at all this chocolate up in here! This is how a woman is supposed to wake up in the morning! And Mo-

Mo? Looks like you all excited this morning! Put that thing away, before you hurt somebody!"

Vernon and I are cracking up laughing as Mo-Mo quickly turns, and disappears out the doorway.

Pretty Kevin just looks at Vernon and me. "Oh, so y'all got jokes this morning! I like your style, sistah. You're all that and a bag of chips. But don't get too cocky up in here. I'd hate to have to spank that ass!"

"Can I watch?" St. Louis Slim asks as Agent Duvall gives him a sarcastic smirk.

She goes up and pinches St. Louis Slim on the cheek. "Sure, you can watch me spank Pretty Kevin's ass, sugar. That'll turn me on too," she says, smiling at Pretty Kevin.

We all burst out laughing.

Pretty Kevin taps his feet on the floor gazing at all of us with a blank expression. "That shit ain't funny, she just flipped the script. All right, Brown Sugar, you got me on that one, but watch your back, Sweet Mama; I might be sneaking up on ya."

"Promises-promises," Agent Duvall responds.

The fellas shut their door to get dressed. Vernon grabs his things and goes into the bathroom, while I fill Agent Duvall in on the crucial information on the case and last night's events.

It takes about twenty minutes to give Agent Duvall all the critical information on Dread, our mission on this case, and to see her to the door so she could freshen up for our busy day. Her room was just down the hallway. She asked several questions about Agent Cheryl Chase, but the one that sticks out most is when she asked, "Can Chase be trusted?"

I really never took the time to consider her current state of loyalty. I knew Vernon had his doubts. Sierra certainly was against Chase's loyalty, and I understand that for me to get her out of this mess, I have to believe that she is on the straight and narrow with me. We've been through a lot together on other cases and she came through like a champ. Surely, that wouldn't change.

Now, Agent James is a totally different can of worms. He is one of those people that you know for a long time, but still can't put a finger on what makes him tick. I've never considered him a friend, just an associate. I do have a sense of trust for him. Vernon thinks he's an Uncle Tom who will sell us out if we can't help him with one of his cases that his White FBI agents can't handle.

Agent James has always taken care of us, and has always been a man of his word. If I have to choose between him and Chase in the loyalty department, Chase would win hands down. Maybe that's what Chase counted on when she phoned me? I don't know. Things are crazy, but I have my hunches and my gut instincts are what I trust the most. They've saved Vernon's and my life on multiple occasions. If I know anything, it's to trust my judgments, listen to my instincts, and pray to God that they're right.

I think of my father and what it must feel like to know you are going to die. Shit. Is this thought symbolic? For all I know, I'm walking into a trap right now. But, if I keep up this thought process; I'll loose focus, and get fucked up in the end. Gotta keep my wits about me.

How does Dad feel knowing that he has to make peace with God and the world in such a short time? How lonely Dad must feel to be in excruciating pain as cancer consumes his body; yet, how comforting it must be to have his family by his side at all times, to reassure him that he's not alone in his transition. What would I be thinking if my time came? What would I say to my children, how would I reflect on my life? What would I say to my wife? What would I say to my brothers, sisters, and friends?

I can hear my dad with a big smile stating his famous words, "Always give a person their flowers while they are still alive, so they can appreciate them; cause flowers don't mean shit when you're dead."

I have to get back to my father and tell him how much he means to me, and how much I love. I have to make sure I give him his flowers, while he's still able to appreciate them. I wipe the tears swelling up in my eyes as Vernon enters the room.

"You all right, partner?" he asks unwrapping a cigar and putting it into his mouth.

I stand up and adjust my clothes. "Yeah, I'm cool. Just reminiscing."

"Joe, we'll get back in time for you to talk with your dad. Right now, let's talk about this Dread fella. You know he will have us walking into a trap."

"Yeah, He knows the area and if he has us driving, he'll probably try and knock us off one-by-one. I'll call and have Agent James have an FBI helicopter on stand-by at the Omaha airport. They should be able to get to us within minutes of our call. We'll need a gunner in the air to assist us. We can handle this and see where it leads."

"That sounds like a good plan to me."

"Thanks for your friendship, Vernon. I'm glad you're with me on this."

"You my dawg, Joe. That's what friends and partners do. They have each other's back through thick and thin. Come on. Get your shit, so we can get your hoodlum friends and eat breakfast before we go see Dread."

I grab the briefcase that has Dread's men's badges and guns in it, put on my suit jacket, call the fellas and Agent Duvall's room, and head for the lobby of the hotel.

twelve

CHASE ONLY CONSIDERED SUICIDE ONCE BEFORE. WHEN HER parents died. She felt like she had lost the world. This morning brings the same morbid feelings of depression and hopelessness. Last night with Dread still has her nauseated. She contemplated abandoning the case when she had the chance, but she has a job to do. Her orders are to bring down Dread no matter what the cost. She struggles with the death and murders of others and feels she should have stopped them if it meant her own life, but Agent James had discussed with her that there would be friendly-fire casualties. Men involved in the black-ring knew their risk.

She finds herself in a fetal position. The only thing she knows is that she's not considering just her death; she will take Dread with her. Her only fear is damnation. She knows she's not perfect. Shit, she's in love with a married man. But she was taught that life is God's gift, and to take it for selfish reasons would result in damnation. So suicide is not an option.

"Chase, you need to get up, darling. I've already called in for us, but we got to gets da' badges back from dat Kansas City prick Detective. He does not know who he fucks wit'. I will call him dis morning and set up an accident. I will make sure he brings the guns and da' badges. I admire dis Johnson. He would make a good adversary, I think," Dread says as he dries his black hair with his bath towel, leaving himself exposed.

How to warn Joe of this imminent danger?

"Dread, wouldn't it be easier to bring him on board? A person this elusive and resourceful could be good for your organization, don't you think?"

Dread stops drying his hair and tilts his head raising his eye-brows in surprise. "I thought of dat, yes, but I have to teach dis guy a lesson for fucking wit' my men. An example has to be made. Yes, an accident is in dis guy's near future. I feel da' urge to burn somebody up. I should have burned dat rat bastard, Smelly, that worked for da' FBI. You get dressed, meet me and da' boys downstairs, and we can set dis' up. After we do dis, we'll go to Kansas City and get away for a couple of days. We'll spend some time in da' Plaza area you like so much. You got twenty-five minutes," Dread orders as he leaves the room.

She thinks of Smelly, and fear engulfs her body. She has to warn Joe somehow. She grabs her cell phone, rushes into the bathroom, and locks the door behind her. She turns on the shower and calls Agent James.

"Agent James, here," he answers.

She gathers her nerves, nervous energy still edges her every word. "They're planning to kill Detective Johnson. You have to warn him. Dread is going to set up a bogus meeting and try to drive them off the road. He'll probably try to burn his body like the others!"

"Just calm down, Agent Chase. I know this is a trying time, but Johnson is very resourceful. He's already called in and we have a helicopter on stand-by in Omaha. Have you retrieved the information we talked about yet?"

"Did you hear what I just said? They're going to kill Johnson!" She sternly says into the phone.

After a pause he replies, "Agent Chase, do you think it'll do us any good if Johnson is killed and we don't have that information on the black ring? I heard you loud and clear. Now, did you hear me? We need to know who is pulling Dread's strings. You do whatever you can do to make sure Detective Johnson is not killed without blowing your cover. Get that information so we can get you out of this mess, and take that asshole down. You got me, Agent?"

She slumps against the bathroom door, tears running down her face.

"Yes, I got it!" She hangs up, and hides the phone in her closet. She takes off her panties and bra, and gets into the hot shower thinking of her next move.

***

She enters the kitchen in her mother's old Paine College sweat shirt and a pair of blue jeans. The whole crew is seated around the table, drinking coffee and eating bagels.

"Bout time, baby. I was beginning to worry 'bout you,"
Dread complained.

Chase just sat down and poured herself a cup of hot coffee. Brutus winked at her, and the others acted like I wasn't even there.

Dread pulls out his cell phone, dials Joe's number, and places his cell on speakerphone.

"Johnson, here."

Chase wants to melt when she hears his deep voice. She bites her tongue to keep from screaming out to him that he is in danger and is being set up.

"Johnson, dis is Dread Cattanno. My men tell me that you are interested in meeting wit' me? I was impressed wit' your resourcefulness last night. You have something you need to return to my men, no?"

"Yes, I do, and I'd love to meet with you. I just didn't understand why I got such a welcome from you? I was just coming down here to make some quick cash and you're the man to make that happen."

"Well, I'm sorry bout' dat, but you don't come wit' references, now do you? But, enuff of dis small talk. Do you like history, Detective?" Dread asks.

"It all depends."

"Have you heard of Scotts Bluff off on Highway 26? It's where the Horse Creek Treaty was signed by da largest gathering of Indians in American history. The treaty was signed to ensure safe passage of west-ward-bound pioneers, and to end tribal warfare within da Native American Indian tribes. Meet us at da crest of Scotts Bluff. You are not to worry. It's a tourist attraction, so there will be lots of folks around."

"Okay, Scotts Bluff it is. When do you want to meet?"

Dread looks at his watch. "There's no time like da' present," Dread says checking his finger nails. "Let's say in one hour."

"I'll see you there."

Dread hangs up his phone. "Like a fly in a spider's web! He's set up just like dat."

His men get up from the table and head toward the drive. Chase admires Joe. She's never known him to back down from anything, but he's gotten in over his head. He's never met anyone like Dread before.

She grabs her Styrofoam cup and pours some more hot coffee into it. More than one "accident" is about to take place today. She realizes that Joe is her only hope of getting out of this alive.

She sits back at the table and waits on Dread as he looks up at the ceiling running his hands through his hair pondering something. He picks his cell phone back up and dials a number. He winks at her as she sips her coffee. He turns to the men who are checking their new weapons and loading additional rifles into the SUV's.

"Dread, do I have to go?"

He jerks up his hand to stop my conversation as he speaks into the phone. "It's me. Yes, I am to meet wit' him in about an hour. I will get da' badges and guns back." He pauses and puts his hand in his pocket, while shifting his weight. "Yes, I agree, someone will have to be made an example of. It will take place at Scott's Bluff." He frowns. "What do you mean not to burn the bodies? Dis is what I do!" He rolls his eyes in frustration as he paces. "I know it's a public place, that's why I chose it, I did not want to make him suspicious." He sighs heavily. "Okay, I will do what you wish, but I feel very uncomfortable about dis. I will call you when it's done. I will be in Kansas City for a few days after dat'. You know how to contact me? Okay. Later." Dread hangs up the phone and turns to me. "What were you saying, my dear?"

"I asked is it necessary for me to come today? I'm feeling like I'm about to start my period. I'm cramping really bad."

"Well, you need to hurry and grab some pads and pain pills, 'cause you will be coming today," he answers, shaking his head, blushing.

She walks upstairs and comes back down to the kitchen where he is waiting by the door. "So, Dread, who was that you were just talking to? You're giving me the impression you're answering to somebody."

He takes a step towards her and she backs up.

"It's none of your fucking business who I talk wit, and since when you start fucking around in my business? Dread answers to no one. He's an advisor. That's all you need to know. Now go get in da' fuckin' truck!"

She does as told. It seems that Joe will at least be able to live another day. Somebody has given Dread the order not to kill and burn him. Please God, let Vernon not be with him. Joe will not know how to act if something happens to his partner. Someone will surely die if that happens. Dread is playing a deadly game and doesn't even know it.

thirteen

WE DRIVE ALONG THE LONG STRETCHING ROADS OF HIGHWAY 29. Vernon and I are in the Corvette. Driving behind us are Pretty Kevin and Mo-Mo in the front seat of their Suburban, along with Little Tiny, Sweet St. Louis, and Agent Duvall, who are all sitting in the back.

The sun is up in the brilliant blue skies revealing God's wonders of lush green mountains, assorted colored birds dashing around like they are playing tag and happy that freedom is the air that keeps them in flight, cattle mulch on the wild grass in the vast fields, horses lazily wonder about with an occasional gait as the magnificent animals seem to dance in groups as they change direction at a moments notice milling about, and a few wild prairie dogs stick their heads out nervously here and there as they run from one hole to another.

The warm wind is soothing. I adjust my sunshades and enjoy the music of Santana. Vernon turns to me and lowers the volume of the music. "Joe, you think it might be a symbolic reason why Dread chose Scott's Bluff for a meeting place?"

I rub my eye-brow and bite my bottom lip. "It's where the Indians signed the treaty for safe passage of the pioneers."

"That's my point. That treaty was broken in less than two days by the pioneers. Have you ever known of any treaty that the white man has honored? This is a trap, partner. They're probably getting us up in these here mountains to ambush us," Vernon says as he grabs a rifle and a hand full of the small explosives out of the back compartment, then tightens his seat belt.

I have always admired Vernon's reasoning and knowledge. He makes sense. Dread is setting us up, probably to get the badges and guns back. I'm glad I've already called Agent James and notified him to dispatch the FBI helicopter to this area for back-up. This guy is really starting to piss me off. I pull out my cell phone and call pretty Kevin to warn him.

When I hang up and look out of my side mirror, I see two black SUV's speeding toward us. They are less than a quarter of a mile from the curve we just passed. My cell phone rings.

"Johnson, speaking!"

"Detective Johnson, Agent James. Chase called and said that you guys are driving into a trap. The copter was dispatched fifteen minutes ago and they currently have you guys in sight. You are being followed. I gave them permission to engage."

"Well, it's a little late for that. These guys are on our asses as we speak."

"Be careful, Johnson. Do whatever you can to evade the situation," Agent James orders.

"Well, seeing that our only evasive alternative is a five mile drop off the side of the mountain, I think I'll take your advice."

I flip the phone closed and pick up speed. Pretty Kevin is right behind me. We take the curves at over sixty miles an hour. I continually check the rear view. Gunfire pops and Pretty Kevin ducks as Little Tiny and Agent Duvall fire shots from either side of the vehicle.

From the horizon of the cliff the gray and blue FBI helicopter appears as a rocket blasts into the side of the mountain right above the on coming black SUV"s that quickly maneuver around the large falling rocks and dirt.

Vernon loads the rifle and cocks it. "Can you move this piece of shit any faster, Joe? We need to make some space between them and us, before those FBI boys bury all of us on this mountain."

"Shut up, with your old ass. You think you can do better? Shit, I'm doing a hundred and ten! I can't control the car on these curves if I go any faster."

Vernon takes out a cigar, unwraps it, and puts it in his mouth. He looks at me, removes the cigar, and holds it between his fingers. "I ain't gonna take too many more of your old ass jokes, nigga. When we get out of this, remind me that I owe you an ass whippin'."

"Vernon, can you stop fuckin' with me long enough for me to drive this car? Damn, man. There's a time and a place to be jive talkin', and now ain't the time. Okay?"

"Whatever!" Vernon responds as he puts his cigar back in his mouth and readies his rifle as another blast from the copter hits the side of the mountain.

Pretty Kevin's SUV swerves from the rubble and goes off the road in a cloud of dust.

"They got Pretty Kevin, Vernon! His car just went off the road!"

We look back. Out of nowhere, the two black SUV's burst through the dirt cloud and give chase. Another blast from the helicopter hits the mountain and slows down on of the black Sport Utility Vehicles. Smoke is coming from the FBI helicopter. It has taken a hit from the other Suv that is gaining on us. The large copter spins in the air out of control with its blades sputtering and starts falling towards us.

"Aim for their tires, Vernon, and see if we can get them off our ass! That helicopter is about to take us all out."

"I'm on it," Vernon says as he leans out the window. He throws the explosives, which detonate, but not in time to do any damage to the vehicles. He pulls out the rifle and starts blasting at the truck's tires.

Shots ring back from the SUV, and both Vernon and I duck inside as a bullet comes through the back window and exits through the windshield.

"Damn-it! Those motherfucker's are shooting back!"

I look at Vernon as I steer the Corvette on the mountain's curve. The helicopter hits the side of the mountain and explodes as rocks, metal debris, and dirt are thrown over the road. A mass hunk of steel falls from the sky and over the edge of the mountain. We hear thumps on the roof and see pieces of rubble bounce off the hood of the car. I pick up speed. The car handles beautifully until an SUV crashes into the back of us. Vernon and I are thrust forward. Rubber from the tires burning, gasoline and smoke scents fill the car as I pump the brakes and try to control the vehicle. An explosion roars as our tire gets shot out. We go into a quick fishtail swerve. The air bags deploy.

I pull my pistol and shoot the airbag. The car falls forward.

"Motherfucker you shot me in the foot!" Vernon yells.

"Shit, I'm sorry Vernon!" I try to steer the car down the side of the mountain, dodging trees and rocks. We crash into a boulder.

Something wet oozes from my head. I'm becoming very dizzy. I look at Vernon. Out cold. His left arm is in the weirdest position. It must be broken.

Someone's arm pushes me to the side. The bag that we used to hide the guns and badges of Dread's men is pulled from the backseat of the Corvette. A crashing thud blasts the side of my face.

"Who has the last laugh now, asshole?" is all the assailant says.

I lay my head on the steering wheel and don't even mind that the horn is blaring. I slowly black out.

***

I am sitting on the front porch with my father, eating salted shelled peanuts, and listening to the Kansas City Royals game on the radio - two of my dad's favorite past times.

"What are you about, son?" he asks with the glint of mystery in his eyes.

I think about my dad's question, and know he is trying to have me look inside of myself. He often does this when he wants to teach me about manhood.

"Can you be more specific, Dad?"

He picks the two peanuts out of the half shell and pops them into his mouth. He licks the salt off his fingers after dropping the shell into the pile that grows at his feet.

"What do you stand for, boy? What makes you different from this peanut I hold in my hand?" He cracks open two more peanuts.

"I have a soul, mind, conscious, and free will. I am made in God's own essence. I exist to make a difference in life, to affect someone other than myself on my road to try to be the best that I can," I answer.

My father's face lights up as a smile spreads across his face. He picks up his tall glass of Kool-Aid and takes a long drink. "A lot of people know how to start something, but not many know how to finish. Always finish what you start. Have a word, and be a friend that a man would die for. Respect yourself and your family, or life won't mean shit. Always remember that, son."

My father places his hand on my leg and squeezes it. "You know I've always been proud of you, son. You've been good to me. I could always talk to you. You had your moments where I had to whip that ass a few times, but you came out all right. I love you, boy. You always remember that, Joe. You're my baby boy, a chip off the old block. You do what you got to do to make things right and everything else will work out fine."

Tears swell in my father's eyes and I feel proud to be his offspring.

"Dad, I saw all those times where you only put ten dollars in your wallet after pay day and gave Mother the rest to take care of the bills. Things were tight, but y'all made us feel like we were rich. Y'all took us out of town, to baseball games, gave us birthday parties and barbecues in the park. You prayed with us at night and made sure we got our school work done. You made sure we could read, even though you were denied that right. I would not have wanted anyone else for a father. I love you and wish I could be half the man you are, Daddy. Thanks for giving yourself unselfishly and showing me what a father should be."

My Dad looks at me, nods, smiles, and winks. There is a silence of respect and admiration shared between us that words will only stiffen. My father stands up and I do, too. He hugs me and smiles, and shakes his head with pride and walks into the house. I sit down on the steps and finish a few more peanuts. A few minutes later, I scoop up all the shells from our baseball feast and throw them into the trash can on the porch. I finish my drink, grab Dad's glass, and try to go into the house, but the door is locked. I struggle to open the door, but it won't open. I want to be with my father!

***

"Johnson, you all right, dawg?" Pretty Kevin asks as I try to adjust to the lights in the room.

"What?" I question, groggy from the pain.

"Dude, you got knocked out after you guys crashed into that boulder, man. You're in the hospital. You've been out for about four hours, dawg. You were mumbling some weird shit about your dad. You must a been dreaming, dude," Pretty Kevin explains.

I look around the pastel blue room. An I-V bottle and rack is placed next to my bed, along with the EKG machine that intermittently beeps as it keeps track of my heartbeat. I think of the dream of my father. What's the lesson?

Over by the window Agent Jason "Little Tiny" Phillips gives me a nod and a small smile, then looks at the ground in front of him. Agent Epiphany Duvall is holding Mo-Mo, who is in tears. They almost look intimate. They make a good couple, but I only been out for four hours. They could not have gotten that close in such a short time.

Besides Mo-Mo's never gotten so close to a woman that he would openly cry in front of her. Something feels strange about this whole thing. Am I dreaming again?

I check the other side of the room and see Vernon in the other bed. He rolls his eyes at me, but manages to crack me a small smile. Thank God we're both okay and he still has a sense of humor. His arm is in a cast, and his bandaged foot is hanging from the ceiling. He winks at me and I know that all is well with us, even though I shot him in the foot.

But something is not right. A gloom has filled the room, like a cloud cast over the sun on a beautiful day, like mud on a white suit. Something has been ruined or destroyed.

It makes me think of my cousin Mervin, who has been a convict most of his life. He used to get into arguments with people and they would turn violent. He would set two pistols out on the table, put his hands up, and dare the other man to shoot him with one of them. If the man didn't try to take the gun and backed away, he would live.

But, if a man made the mistake of letting his emotions get the best of him, Mervin would quickly pull a pistol from the small of his back and shoot. This way he could plead self-defense. He always thought this was fair, although he failed to mention to the men that the two guns he set on the table were not loaded.

He would later explain that a man who can't control his emotions, didn't deserve a fair shot at life. He would say that life ain't fair, so you best do something about it, and to not let life lead you, but you must lead life. Almost killed at the age of forty-five in a gun fight, Mervin is a preacher now, and his mission is saving lives. He has a Baptist church on Quindaro Boulevard in Kansas City, Kansas. Life has a way of catching up with you and evening the score.

I search the room once again; then realize who it is I don't see. Sweet St. Louis Slim.

"Joe, Sweet St. Louis didn't make it. He was shot in the head by a stray bullet," Vernon explains as his deep brown eyes swell with sorrow and grief looking at Mo-Mo. He returns his gaze to me.

The anti-septic smell of the room is thickened by the death and mourning. Depression dulls the spirit in everyone's eyes, but with a hard edge of vengefulness. More people are gonna die behind this black ring of dirty cops. One thing is understood from my band of childhood friends: No one dies in vain, and no one gets away with killing a friend.

I feel like my guts have been pulled out, and anger begins to boil in the depths of my existence. My friend sacrificed his life to help me. I thought for sure that the helicopter could have taken them out or that we would have been able to overpower them in a meeting. I think of Sierra and can hear her asking me if Chase is worth it. I bite my lower lip as tears of anger and sorrow roll down my face.

"Mo-Mo, I'm so sorry, dude." I reach out my hand to him and he takes it, and embraces me.

He says in my ear. "Joe, he was the best friend I had in the whole world, man. He was my family. What am I gonna do now, dawg? What am I gonna do?" he asks, breaking down crying.

Agent Epiphany Duvall comes to put her arms around Mo-Mo. Her hazel eyes are filled with love and devotion, it even melts my emotions. I don't know if Mo-Mo realizes or even knows how lucky he is to have a woman by his side at a time like this.

One thing I learned from seeing my father and mother is that with a strong woman behind you, there ain't nothing you can't get through, or do. A strong woman will lift you up when you are at your lowest point. Her love gives your heart reason to live, when you feel like dying. She can make you feel like the most important man in the world; even when the world says you're insignificant.

A woman can make you believe in the Holy Ghost, when you question God about how hard life is. She can give you a glimpse of heaven with her love making. She can make a cardboard shack feel like a palace. A strong woman is a powerful thang. I know my friend will be all right, cause by the way Agent Duvall touches him, I know she has already breathed life into him, and claimed him for her own.

"We're your family now, baby. You won't be alone," she says to my sorrow-torn friend.

Vernon raises the head part of his bed with the remote that is hooked on the railing, which prevents him from rolling out of bed.

"Joe, the doctor is transferring me to Kansas City later today. I think you need to come back with me. We need to regroup. We can get with Commissioner Wayne and get some help on this. You can trust him, you know that," he says.

I think of what my father would always say, "Never take out your gun, unless you plan to use it. And always finish what you start."

I knew Vernon should not have come, I feel awful that he is hurt, but it's best that he go back. Maybe God did this for a reason.

"Vernon, if the trail leads me back to Kansas City, that's where I'll go, but I have to finish this." I turn to face Jason 'Little Tiny' Phillips, Pretty

Kevin, Agent Duvall, and Mo-Mo. "Look, I thank you guys for helping me, but it's personal now, and I won't ask any of you to put your life on the line for this case. Mo-Mo, I'll have the rest of your money for you by the end of the day. It's at the hotel. Pretty Kevin, I have money for you as well. I appreciate what y'all have done. I can take it from here."

Vernon rolls his eyes at me, and claps his hands in disgust. "Joe, got-damn-it, boy. You just don't get it, do you? You done shot me in the foot, now you gonna put me and your friends down like yesterday's potatoes." Vernon snarls with bitter disappointment on his face and his lower lip quivering with anger.

Pretty Kevin goes over to Vernon and puts his hands on his shoulder to calm him down. "I got this, Vernon." Kevin walks over to my bed and sits at the foot. "Joe, everybody here in this room is here for a reason and it has nothing to do with money. You have put your life on the line for us at one point or another. You always talking this God and Jesus stuff, and I'm starting to wonder if you think that you are an exception to God's plan. Fate brought us all here for a purpose, to save all our souls. They got some bad things going on here, and if we can help make it right, maybe we'll all get some goody points with The Man upstairs. We're friends. You been there for me, and I'm damn sure gonna be there for you." Pretty Kevin thumps me on the big toe.

Little Tiny stands eating the crackers that came with the tomato soup and sipping the apple juice the orderly had brought for me and Vernon's lunch. Mo-Mo is sitting on the heating unit in front of the window that displays white clouds rolling past the blue sky. Agent Duvall sits in the ugly orange visitor's chair with her big legs crossed, her gaze occasionally checking on Mo-Mo.

"Joe, we're your friends, brother. And you don't have to do shit alone. We got into this with you and we're gonna see you out of it. So, Vernon will go back to Kansas City and see what he can find out with your Police Commissioner, and we'll try and get your friend, Agent Chase out. Sweet St. Louis Slim would want it that way, and I got some payback to give."

Little Tiny interjects.

Agent Duvall says, "Joe, I already have new vehicles. The guns that were in the Corvette trunk compartment have been transferred to a yellow Range Rover. It's in the parking lot. The Corvette is in the FBI impound. This's more than an assignment, it's personal now. I've arranged for Vernon to be flown to Kansas City. His wife, Gertrude will be meeting us at the airport."

Vernon adds, "Joe, I know I have always had my particulars about these here fellas, but, I would want them if I was in it thick, because they loyal. You find that Dread, bring his ass down, and get Chase out."

I never thought I'd hear those words come out of Vernon's mouth. He finally sees what I've seen in my friends for years. We are as thick as thieves.

Little Tiny walks up to the bed and addresses us. "Man, I don't have that many black friends; you know me being white and all, shoot I don't have that many friends for that matter, but you guys have accepted me as I am, and Joe, you kept me from getting slapped around too much by Dread's men. I'd go through hell for you and your friends. I'm in, dude."

I inhale deeply. "It's settled then. We'll finish the case together. I appreciate all of you guys. Mo-Mo, we'll get Sweet St. Louis's body flown to St. Louis, and we'll get in contact with his parents."

"Thanks Joe, you can fly his body, but I think his parents would rather hear about this from me. I'll handle that part." Mo-Mo leaves the room to make the call, Agent Duvall right behind him.

The room phone rings and we look at each other. Is Dread calling to fuck with me? I answer the phone on the second ring.

"Detective Johnson, please."

"Agent James, how did you know I was here?"

"I talked with Agent Chase and she told me about the accident. I had my secretary call around to the hospitals there to find where you were admitted to. Are you and Vernon all right? I didn't know he'd be with you."

"We got bruised up a little bit, but we'll be okay."

"Joe, Chase says they're on their way to Kansas City. She has the address book with the list of all the dirty cops. Dread is working with someone… if you can go to his house and rifle through his things, you might be able to see who he is working with?"

"Naw, I think I have a faster way of finding who he is working with. If you talk with Chase again, have her get that book to the Kansas City Homicide unit. I'll have Vernon go through it. I have a hunch."

"Will do. She's been calling in almost daily. They'll be staying at the Hyatt Regency Hotel, off McGee Avenue, down by Crown Center Plaza. She said they were motorcycling down on Harleys."

"Dread's bike of choice. Good to know. Who do you think he's reporting to?"

"I'm really not sure, but it has to be someone who has power, can influence the federal and state police force, plus, have enough savvy and connections to keep a man like Dread in check."

What Agent James just said makes sense, but what he left out is this person would have a hell of a lot to lose, if exposed. They are killing cops, so the penalty would be severe. I don't care how much money and power you have, that's something you can't walk away from or buy yourself out of.

"Agent James, I'll call you when I get to Kansas City," I say and hang up.

Vernon looks at me and raises his bushy eye brows. "You think Agent James is pulling our strings and covering his ass? He would be in an excellent position to get rich, have us kill his man Dread, destroy the evidence, and life would be sweeter than a crack-head that won the lottery."

"Yeah, but a crack-head that won the lottery would be dead in a week from an overdose. It doesn't make sense." I shake my head. "Agent James can be strange sometimes, but he's no cop killer."

Pretty Kevin adds, "Yeah, but if Dread is doing all the killing, then all Agent James got to do is collect the money, and sit back like a fat cat."

I shake my head again, "Naw, I just don't see it."

"Joe, you don't think blind men step in shit? Just because you can't see, don't mean it ain't so." Vernon stares hard at me. "Let's get them Doctor's in here, so we can sign out of this place."

"I'll go look for him," Little Tiny says as he heads for the hallway.

I place a call to my friend, Peter Shelvin, who works for the FBI Surveillance Team in Chicago, to get Dread's phone records, then place another call to Jefferson City, Missouri, to see if my hunch is correct.

When I finish my conversation, I grab my clothes out and get dressed to leave the hospital.

fourteen

The ride on the Classic Harley-Davidsons from Nebraska to Kansas City was scenic, exciting, and fun. Dread rides on his 1957 XL Sportster, Brutus on his 1948 Panhead, Chase has the 1966 Shovelhead, Weasel and Ronnell drive by on their 1986 FLST Softtails. The guys like to play on the road. They are like big kids. But Chase's mind and thoughts continue to be on Joe. Did he and Vernon get hurt when they went off the road and crashed down the mountainside? She isn't sure what Brutus did to them when he went to retrieve the bag, but she do know that Dread gave him specific orders not to kill them.

Brutus didn't say much about their condition when he came back up and got into the car. Dread was pleased to have his men's weapons and badges back. He made arrangement's early this morning with the desk sergeant, who's on his payroll, to put all of them on vacation leave for three days.

Funny how no one questions Dread's authority. It seems to be true that 'The love of money is the root of all evil', because these men and women who have sworn to serve and protect their communities will do any and everything for money. And they have.

They check into the luxurious hotel. The white and gray marbled interior, accentuated with glass and gold fixture Hyatt is situated near three historical landmarks. The Union Station/Science Center, which is across the street, houses the train depot and the new Science Center, where they feature traveling museums and a permanent weather station. The Union Station is also famous for the St. Valentine's Day massacre, where Pretty Boy Floyd and Frank Nitty were gunned down by Elliott Ness and his men.

About four blocks away stands the Liberty Memorial, a huge concrete tower with twin museums on either side. An eternal flame at the top is always lit. This museum honors War Veteran's of World War I & II.

Across the street and to the left of the hotel is Crown Center Plaza. It's a futuristic idea of a Metroplex, where employees who worked at the center in the office buildings never had to leave the area for shopping, entertainment, or dining. One can get to all of these locations and not even venture outside, because they are all connected by a suspended walkway.

The Hyatt is a state-of-the-art hotel, but when originally built it had an elevated glass walkway that overlooked the entrance lobby and main ballroom. In the early 90's at a New Year's Eve party, the glass walkway gave way and hundred's of people were killed and thousands more injured. It took several days to extricate people from the rubble.

The hotel is magnificent with its marble floors, brass fixtures and statues, Gothic and Victorian Art, and mahogany wood tables and chairs. Dread checks us in. The men get separate rooms and Dread puts him and Chase in a corporate suite. They all get settled and decide to have an early afternoon lunch at the Hotel's five-star restaurant; the Peppercorn Duck Club.

The host's name tag reads, Myron, a handsome man with bronze skin and clean shaven. He has earrings in both ears, his uniform is perfectly neat, his shirt is a flamingo pink, his hair is permed, styled, and looks better than mine. His fingernails are manicured and have a gloss coat on them.

He strolls up to meet them and looks Dread from head to toe, sucking his teeth, licking his lips, and fanning himself. "Hel<u>lo</u>, my name is Myron. Welcome to the Peppercorn Duck club. How many in your party today, Mr. Sir?"

"Seven, Myron," Dread answers Looking at us and rolling his eyes while blushing.

"Very good. Walk this way please," Myron instructs as he sashays to their table with a little extra snap in his hips for Dread's pleasure.

Chase surveys the half-filled restaurant and sees Detective Joe Johnson's troublesome ex-girlfriend, Tracy Jackson, seated with three female friends. She tries to go unnoticed, but Tracy quickly looks up and gives her an evil gaze. Chase tries to act like she doesn't notice. She swears this woman has to be Satan's child. Tracy works as a television anchor and used to be a reporter, so the last thing Chase wants is for her to start sticking her nose in her business, and mess up this case. She makes sure that her seat is not facing Tracy's in hopes she catches her hint not to bother her.

Their last meeting was not a good one. Chase had to front Tracy on her job in the ladies room, when they needed information and tried to avoid her going public with a story that would have blown the case on which Joe, Vernon, and her were working.

Tracy has been a thorn in Joe's side for several years. He's confided in Chase several times, that at one point he felt like she was stalking him. Chase just hopes she stays where she is, because she's not in the mood for any nonsense.

Chase tries to see if she can get Myron's attention. He sees her wave and comes over from his post.

"My I help you, Ms. Ma'am?"

"Yes, you can. Where is the ladies room?" she looks him deep in the eyes hoping he can get her hint that she wants him to show her where it is.

"Let me show you, if you don't mind," Myron says on cue, winking at her.

She excuses herself and follows Myron to the ladies room. They pass

Tracy's table, and she eyes her. When we get out of Dread's view and by the women's bathroom, she takes Myron's hand.

"Look baby, you might not have noticed, and I know you cute and all, but I am not into women. Don't get me wrong, if I was, you would definitely be my type, girlfriend," he says, smiling.

She grabs Myron by the face. "Shut up Myron, it ain't that kinda party. I need you to take this film and have it taken by courier to the Downtown Police Department, care of Commissioner Wayne for Detective Joe Johnson. Here is three hundred dollars, that should take care of the thirty dollar fee for the courier and you can keep the change for yourself. Not a word of this to <u>anyone</u>." She stares hard at him.

Myron raises his eye brows and leans back with his hand on his chest, "Okay lady, thanks. But, you don't have to be all up in my space, grabbing on me, and shit. Next time just ask, okay?" Myron complains with his well-manicured hands on his slender hips.

Chase kisses Myron on the cheek as he leaves to send off the package and enter the bathroom. By the time she walk to the sink to wash her hands, check her face, and hair in the mirror, Tracy walks up behind her.

She walks up to the mirror, flips her hair, checks her teeth, lips, face, and eyes Chase's reflection as she applies lipstick.

"So, Agent What-cha-ma-call-it, where's your friend, Detective Johnson? He kicked you to the curb, and you decided to go Cuban or <u>what</u>?" she asks with a sneer, snapping her fingers as if she's trying to remember her name.

Chase turns to face her. The bitch. The pissed-off look she gives her makes her back up a little.

"Joe is none of your concern. Furthermore, who I date is none of your damn business. I suggest you stay out of my space and out of my way. You're venturing in dangerous territory, girl. So why don't you just go join your stuck-up friends before you start to piss me off, TV Lady." She brings her face so close to Tracy's, that she can feel her breath on her face.

"You…you…you don't scare me, I know you're hot on Joe, I'm not stupid. It's all over your face. If Joe is going to be with anybody, it's going to be me. So, you need to step off," Tracy says as she rolls her eyes at Chase and sucks her teeth.

Chase wants to haul off and hit her in the face, but can not afford to create a scene with things going so good. She looks at her as tho she's just called her newborn child ugly.

"Look bitch, stay out of my face, and stay out of my way or I promise you, I'll make your life a living hell. Okay Tracy?"

Tracy and Chase just stare at each other for forty seconds. Tracy pivots at the door and holds it open. "I got your bitch, bitch. I know you're up to something and Joe has got to be nearby, but I'll get to the bottom of it. You can count on that." She flicks her hair, rolls her eyes, and leaves the room.

Tracy is trouble. She has what we use to call a graveyard love with Joe; the kind of love a woman will take to her grave. It's an obsessive-compulsive kind of love, but there is much truth in what she is saying. Chase does want Joe for her own. Yes, he's a married man, but she would still settle to just have a piece of him. Although it's wrong, and she likes Sierra, she knows what she wants—Joe Johnson. Tracy's no threat to her and Joe's friendship, but she is as a threat to this case.

She considers calling Agent James, but can't shake the feeling that something is not right with him. Can she trust him? And what are his dealings with the Governor? Could Agent James be on the take and pulling Dread's strings? He could sure have the crooks and the cops chasing each other. They would all be on a line and he could play them like puppets against each other. They kill each other off, and he walks away never a suspect, and with all the cash. That's a sweet plan, but Chase is not about to be played.

She returns to the table where the men are talking, laughing, eating appetizers, and having drinks. Tracy stares at her from the other table and she can see her whispering to her friends as they all laugh and begin to cut their eyes at her. Chase ignores them.

Dread looks at her, and then at the women, "Is everything okay? Are those friends of yours or somethin'?"

Chase glances at Dread and then back at the menu, "Naw, she's just some stupid reporter that had got too close to a case I'd been working on early in my career. I had to check her. She's hasn't got over it, and is still being silly about it, that's all."

Dread places his hand on hers, "Do you want me to go over dar' and shut them up for you?" Dread strokes her hair.

"Dread, I can handle my own battles and she is not worth it. I'm fine," She says taking her hand from under his and places her order.

Dread looks over at the table smiles and gives them the finger as the men at the table start laughing. People around them look to see what the laughter is about, but Chase pulls down Dread's finger and they continue as if nothing had happened.

After they eat, Dread passes envelopes to all the men that contain ten thousand dollars for each of them. He says they should spoil themselves at the Plaza in Midtown Kansas City. They are to meet in the lobby in one hour. Chase will try to get a chance to call Joe's and Vernon's office, as well as Commissioner Wayne's, to tell them where she will be. Hopefully, they'll check their messages.

fifteen

VERNON CALLS ME FROM MY PARENTS' HOME. HE IS A TRUE friend and instead of going home to mend his own wounds, he and Agent Duvall goes to my father's. He tells me my dad is not doing well, and I should get there as soon as possible. I promise him that I will.

The day is beautiful, full of sunshine and blue skies, with temperature in the mid-seventies. I check to make sure that Pretty Kevin, Little Tiny, and Mo-Mo can drive motorcycles and then when we get into downtown Kansas City we go to the Federal Bureau of Investigation vehicle impound garage. We trade the SUV in for bikes. It makes sense to travel as Dread travels. That way no obstacles or barriers exist if we need to get to them.

I get the 2002 VRSCA V-Rod Harley-Davidson and the others all get the 2002 FXSTDI Softail Deuce Motorcycles. I sign the paper work and we get helmets. Then we drive to my parents' home to meet Vernon and my family, so I can check on my dad.

Our ride from the tall glass plated buildings and windy streets of downtown to my parents' home, is pretty cool. It's been some time since I last rode a motorcycle. It gives you a sense of freedom and the open air consumes you. We ride in formation, two by two. Me and Pretty Kevin followed by Little Tiny, Epiphany Duvall, and Mo-Mo.

I took the liberty of unloading the guns from the Range rover and transferring them to each of our saddle bags straddled on the back of our Harleys. I have a feeling that Dread is in town and if he is, I know a show down is inevitable. I plan to be ready.

We arrive at my parents' three-story, white, stone-masoned home and park the bikes in front on the wide sidewalk. When we enter Sierra jumps into my arms, and squeezes me tight. Her eyes are sad, but her smile is beautiful. The kids are close behind and they all take hold of me. Vernon waves the fellas into the kitchen, where I'm sure more of my family is. I introduce the fellas to my wife and family as they pass us.

"Friends, this is my lovely wife, Sierra, and these are my kids, Vernie, Joe Jr., and Nia. Oh-oh, where'd you come from?" I ask my little nephew-in-law, Raymond Tyler, Jr. as I pick him up and hug him.

"I came wit' Mommy," he answers, smiling from ear to ear. I put him down, so he can be with the other children as they run from the room.

Raymond Jr. and Nia are really brother and sister. We adopted Nia from Sierra's mom, Ebony Dupree, when she was incarcerated for the death of her lover, Raymond Tyler. Sierra's twin sister, Diamond, and Ebony were both seeing Raymond at the same time, but they didn't know. They both got pregnant by him. Raymond was my high school best friend. Nia and Raymond, Jr. were born three days apart. Raymond Jr., the eldest of the two, is also Nia's Uncle.

"Family, you guys know Pretty Kevin, this here is Mo-Mo, the big guy here is Little Tiny, and the beautiful lady is Agent Epiphany Duvall," I say.

"Nice to meet you nice people," Little Tiny says as he shakes all their hands and continues into the kitchen.

I turn to my wife. "How's Dad?"

Sierra buries her head in my chest and holds me tight. "Not doing too good, Joe. His system is slowly shutting down. He hasn't opened his eyes in thirty hours, but he can flare his nostrils and raise his eyebrows to let you know he hears you. Joe, he's lost a lot of weight and they have him wearing an adult diaper. I just didn't want you to be shocked by his appearance, baby. I know it will be hard for you to see him like this," she looks at me with sulking eyes and pulls me close into her embrace.

"Sierra, I just want to tell you how much I appreciate and love you for being here with my family. You mean the world to me, and I promise to never let you down, baby. I'm nothing without you. I needed to tell you that." I kiss my wife.

Sierra's twin sister, Diamond, comes downstairs and we embrace. "Hey Brother-in-law, your mom is asking for you upstairs."

I grasp my wife's hands and kiss her on the cheek, then go up the stairs and head toward my parents' bedroom. I feel like someone has taken a sledgehammer and hit me in the chest.

On my first hunting trip with my father, I almost stepped on top of a copperhead. My father grabbed me and pulled me back and simultaneously cocked the rifle with one hand and fired the twelve-gauge rifle, ripping the snake into several pieces.

I remember the first time I saw my father cry, when his mother died. He went into the dark hallway bathroom and let his emotions pour out of him. I sat next to him on the edge of the tub, put my arm around him, told him that she was with God, and that everything would be okay. I remember how he pulled me to him and cried on my shoulder. We were best friends after that.

At our family barbecues, he'd gather us all together to compete with another family in a softball game. My dad would always be the pitcher. He was good, too. Dad was good about bringing people together to have fun. He has a good heart.

My brothers and sisters hug me as they leave the room to give me and Dad some time alone.

Mom walks up to me. "Joseph, I'm glad you're home and safe, baby. Your father doesn't have much time left with us. They're giving him pure morphine for the pain and to keep him comfortable. You know he loves you, son. Talk to him. Tell him how you feel, because this might be your last opportunity to do so. We'll all be downstairs if you need us. I'll check on you in a few minutes." Mom kisses me on the forehead and leaves the room.

I go to my father's bedside. My heart just dies. I can't help but wish it were me lying there instead of him. He is a shell of himself, but an aura of strength radiates his body. He looks regal. His skin seems to be darker, and his muscles have receded and rest lazily upon his bones. I kiss my dad on the cheek and rub his head.

My body feels full and the tears begin to flow as I hug this man I love so much. I lean over and talk to him.

"Dad, what can I say that you don't already know? I'm glad that you are my father, you did everything for me and you taught me how to love life and myself. You are my best friend in the world and I'm so very proud of you and what you are to this family. Thank you for the love you've given. I know you're in pain. We'll take care of each other, Daddy. When you are ready, go ahead and cross over. You've fought long enough and it's time for you to rest." I am on the verge of breaking down.

When I look up, all my brothers, sisters, my wife, family, friends, and family friends have formed a circle around Dad's bed and are holding hands. I take my mom's and Sierra's hands. Mom leads us in prayer, and we each take turns saying our favorite memory of Dad and how much he means to us. We laugh, cry, and pray. After thirty minutes Dad's eyes open, he looks around the room, smiles, and takes his last breath.

Dad was surrounded by his family, and crossed over with his roses, while he was still alive. We call the Hospice representative who has been working with our family. She comes over, takes Dad's vitals, and calls the coroner. They come out and take his body from our home.

The hardest moment I have ever been through is when they take my father out the front door. He will never come home again. All my brothers watch in the street as the coroner pulls away and we cry like babies. We sit on the steps in front of the house with our wives and friends and tell stories about Dad to comfort ourselves.

I sit on the concrete stairs amongst my brothers, staring up at the cloud formations in the blue afternoon sky. I make out a cloud formation of a small elephant. It makes me think of peanuts and how the elephant and my dad love them in the shell. My father prefers them salted. I smile as my cell phone rings.

"Joe, this is Commissioner Wayne. I received a package for you from FBI Agent Chase. Enclosed was some film we had developed, and we got the names of all the dirty cops. I sent a copy of the list to Internal Affairs and they're in the process of arresting the officers and agents now. We also noticed that Dread has tickets to Cuba, so we took the liberty of canceling his flight arrangements. Agent Chase has a note that she is staying at the Hyatt Regency, but will be at the Plaza this afternoon."

My heart begins to race. If Chase is here, Dread is here. Is his accomplice in town as well? I look at my watch. Close to 2 in the afternoon. Dread must have been getting ready to make his move and leave for Cuba.

"Commissioner Wayne, I just lost my dad, but I'm headed to the Plaza. I'll try and find them. I have an Agent with me for back up. I'll call in if we catch up with them. I'm not sure what cops I can trust to call in for back up, so if you can handpick some of the guys you feel you can trust, and have them wait for my call, I'd appreciate it."

"Joe, I'm sorry about your father, my friend. I'll get some men together. Be careful Joe, this Dread is one bad dude. Agent James sent me a copy of his file. I know Vernon has to be with you, you tell him I said to stand down. He can't help you with one bad foot. You know we got to talk about that accident when you get back to the office, right?"

Commissioner Wayne always had a way of knowing what Vernon and I were up to. He has been a great boss, and a better friend. We have all rose through the ranks together. He has had our backs when things got tough, but we've also made him look good with one of the highest-solved murder ratios in the region.

"Yes, Sir. Thanks for the condolences."

"Joe, are you sure you're up to doing this? You just had a death in the family. Your head's got to be clear on this one, son."

"Me and my father had a great relationship and I was able to talk with him before he crossed over. My father is at peace, and I've done all I can do right now. I'm focused, Sir."

"Okay Johnson, but do this by the book. This is some dangerous shit, son."

We hang up and I go to inform Vernon and the others of the new information. I talk to Sierra and let her know that I have to leave again. She doesn't say anything, but by the way she looks at me and kisses me, I know that all is well.

sixteen

I KNOW FROM MY EXPERIENCE WITH CHASE THAT IF THEY ARE shopping, it will be at Sax Fifth Avenue or the Halls store. We pull off onto Linwood Boulevard and head west to Southwest Traffic Way with Agent Duvall following in her SUV. We get to the forty-seventh street turn and ride into the Plaza shopping district. The area is full of shoppers.

The Plaza, an upscale shopping area, is adorned with beautiful water fountains and European architecture. The curvatures of the buildings are pikes at the tops with steeples and clad statues of Roman and Greek gods of marble and gold. The Lobster Pot, Red Dragon, Ruth Chris Steak House, Cheese Cake Factory, Houston's, and other fabulous restaurants are in this area as well as Sax, Halls, Sabastians, Valentino's, Nine West, Abercrobie & Fitch, and Gucci clothiers abound this district. There are as many famous drinking and jewelry stores throughout the district as well. We catch a lot of impressive stares at our classic bikes, but ignore them.

We ride pass Hall's clothier first. No sign of Dread and his men. We travel down three other streets. Jefferson has mostly home furnishing stores like Pier One, Jacobson's, and The Closet Box.

On Washington Street you have the Plaza III Restaurant and Bar, Star Bucks, and The Washington Street-side Café. Madison Avenue hold's the shoe stores such as Stacy Adams, Nina's, Johnston & Murphy, Dillard's, and Neffertiti Shoe Palace.

We find Dread and his men mounting their bikes on Walnut in front of the Seville Square shopping area that holds the movie theater and assorted novelty shops. A cold stare comes our way from Dread and his men. I look him in his cold dark eyes. We both look around, seeing how many people are in this public place. I get off my bike and nod for him to do the same. We meet in the middle of the side walk.

"Dread, you know what has to be done. I would like to do this the easy way. There are a lot of innocent people around. You come quietly and no one gets hurt. Who are you working for?" I question.

"Detective, wat' makes you think I would tell you anything about me? You don't want dis to be a bloody mess wit all des' innocent peoples around do you? We will have to do dis some other time." Dread sneers as he looks me up and down.

I return his look of disdain. "Look Dread, we can work something out, but I have to know who you're working for. Enough blood has been shed. We need to end this."

Dread looks at his men. I glimpse at Chase to see how she's going to play this. Chase is more beautiful than I remembered. I have to admit, that when our eyes meet, she gives me butterflies. Can I count on her to be on our side if something jumps off? Where does her allegiance lie? She's been undercover for such a long period of time.

Something seems different about her. The softness that has always adorned her face is not there. She is still gorgeous, but whatever she's gone through has hardened her. Thank God she's alive and well, though. She gives me a nod with the tilt of her head. She'll handle her part.

Dread motions for his men to start their bikes and Dread and I reach for our guns at the same time. We both hold are guns at our sides not to draw any more attention to ourselves than we already have. I raise my hand for my crew not to go for their guns. Agent Duvall, Little Tiny, Pretty Kevin, and Mo-Mo tense up, but follow my orders.

Dread pulls out his gloves and puts them on. "So Detective Johnson, I see dat you are one resourceful son-of-a-bitch. I like dat. I would really like to go wit' you, but I apologetically have to humbly refuse your offer. You see we have places to go and people to see, my friend!" Dread yells over the hum of the bikes.

"Dread, you're a smart man. I hope you make an intelligent decision here, do you really want a shoot out in a public place or a chase through the middle of the city?"

Dread laughs and spreads his arms wide, looking around. "As you see, my friend, it's a beautiful day to die, and a marvelous day for a ride. I don't give a shit about these people around here. They will be nothing, but casualties of war. It's your call, Detective." He puts on his shades.

I turn to my people as Dread and I mount our bikes, "Okay, Dread is mine, if you have to take them out, do it in a way that bystanders are not in harm's way. Don't hurt Agent Chase, she's one of ours. I have a feeling shit is about to get ugly. Watch yourselves."

Dread takes off and his men follow right behind. We follow them through the Plaza area, traveling at fifty miles an hours. We dodge shoppers with some of Dread's men taking to the sidewalk to avoid capture. When we clear the district Dread's men take aim and start firing upon us and we return the gun fire. They can't aim straight from the moving motorcycles while they steer the bikes. No one is hit.

Dread's men break off into different directions. I motion for Little Tiny, Mo-Mo, and Pretty Kevin to pursue them. Agent Chase breaks off from the pursuit. Agent Duvall follows her.

Dread picks up speed when he gets onto Wornall Road. We reach eighty miles an hour. I catch up to him when we turn onto Ward parkway, a two-lane winding road. Dread fires at me. He misses. I pull out my 9MM and return the fire.

I reach one hundred miles an hour. I come side by side with my assailant. He quickly hits his breaks, crosses the grassy area, and suddenly stops, getting off his bike and motioning for me to do the same. Dread wants to fight and I want to kick his ass. So I stop my bike and oblige him.

I take off my helmet, set it on the seat of the Harley, and walk up to Dread in the middle of the grassy parkway.

"A man of honor should be able to battle, don't you agree, Detective?" Dread asks, smiling as we circle each other.

"Dread, all I know is you got one hell-of-a ass whooping coming. So stop the small talk and handle your business with your punk-ass!"

Dread attack with an upward elbow. I duck and punch him in the side. As his body lowers from the blow, I hit him in the face. Dread spins and kicks my legs from underneath me. I fall backward. As I land, Dread tries to stomp me in the chest. I catch his leg and throw him to the ground.

We both jump up and get into fighting positions. Cars pull over and watch the battle. Dread rushes me and we exchange blows to the face and chest. Both our noses are bleeding. Dread tries to kick me in the chest. I block his punch and knock him to the ground. His head hits the grass. Before he can stand, I pounce on his chest, and hit him in the face.

"I told you, you had an ass whooping coming, but you didn't believe me, did you?" I punch him in the face again. "This is for St. Louis Slim, you piece of shit!" I hit him again.

Dread moans as he grabs a handful of grass and dirt and throws it into my face. I am temporarily blinded as I feel a crushing blow across my face.

"Yes, I killed your friend and I'm going to get away with it too; you fucking asshole!" Dread kicks me in the chest. I fall over from the pain, and swipe the dirt and grass from my eyes.

Dread staggers to his bike, starts it up, and roars off, speeding back down Ward Parkway toward the Plaza area. I quickly get up, put on my helmet, and go after him. I can't afford to have us speeding into the area where civilians are in harm's way. No one else needs to die today, who's not involved in this drama.

I continue to throttle my bike as Dread turns onto Wornall road. I catch him as we near the Greek god Neptune's Fountain on forty-Seventh Street. The long-haired and bearded Neptune rides three large seahorses, water sprouting from their nostrils. Neptune's arm is raised powerfully with his trident, aimed to strike.

The eight thousand pound, cast lead fountain which sits in an oval pool of water. I kick Dread's bike as hard as I can and force him into Neptune. Dread's bike crashes into the concrete base. Dread is thrown into the air and comes to an abrupt stop. Neptune's trident pierces his chest. His bike is now a twisted pile of chrome, rubber, and metal. A small fire has begun. I stop, get off my bike, quickly take off my helmet, fill it with water, and put out the flame.

Blood spills from Dread's chest into the pool. The once clear blue water that sprouts from the horses nostrils slowly turns crimson. A crowd swells. I quickly go to Dread. He is in intense pain, his body convulses violently as a trickle of blood spills from his mouth. His eyes slowly open.

"Dread, you fucked up, dude. I should have let your ass burn up like you did your victims, because your bike surely would have exploded, and it would have turned your ass into bacon bits. It's confession time, Bro. Who's pulling your strings, Dread? Who you working for?"

He grins, spits on my shirt, laughs, then grimaces, and coughs from pain. "You'll never know, you fuckin' cock-a-roach. I'll take dis information to hell wit me," he says as his breathing starts to break.

"So be it, asshole. I have a hunch who it is anyway, so say hello to the devil for me, fucker."

Dread tries to laugh, but his face contorts. Dread's eye's roll into the back of his head, revealing only the white side of his eye balls as the unseen demons snatch his soul from his body. He takes a deep breath and relaxes. He wets and soils himself as his body control gives way with the violent release of life. Justice has been done for Agent Smelly.

When I turn to walk away, Tracy and a Channel Six cameraman are set up and filming. She walks up to me as the crowd thickens.

"So, Detective Killer Joe, I see this is another body count you can add to your case files. Would you like to explain why a Kansas City Police Detective would put so many people in jeopardy, shooting, and having a motorcycle pursuit in a public, well-populated place?" she asks with all the charm and venom of a poisonous snake.

I look at Tracy with disgust. She seems to take pleasure in tormenting me, ever since I dumped her and married Sierra. A scorned lover is a mother-fucker.

I growl at them, "My name is Detective Joe Johnson and I have no comment. Please stay clear of the area or I'll have to arrest you." They both take a step back.

Tracy has labeled me a killer on national television, and I make a mental note to make her pay. I call Commissioner Wayne for back up as other officers arrive. I give them orders to secure the crime scene, then walk to the back of the crowd to meet with Mo-Mo, Pretty Kevin, and Little Tiny. The crowd parts as I walk amongst them. It must be the "don't fuck with me" look on my face.

"Kevin, what's up? Where's Agent Duvall, and what happened to the other men?"

"Well, how you doing too, Joe. Damn, dude, we all shot up and shit and all you can do is start asking for details on shit," Pretty Kevin complains.

"Kevin, I'm sorry brother, but I'm just making sure that everyone is okay. What happened to Chase and the others?"

Little Tiny limps over to Joe rubbing the back of his neck and is bleeding from a gun shot wound to the leg. "Joe, Agent Duvall took after Agent Chase and we haven't heard from her. Them fools we were after didn't know Kansas City too, well. They ended up crashing into brush creek. The police fished them out of the water. They're in custody, but the big Guy named Brutus got away."

Mo-Mo comes up holding his arm, which is also bleeding. "Dude, if we're here to save Chase, why would she run? Agent Duvall set out after her going north on Southwest Traffic-way. This shit doesn't make no sense. If something happens to Epiphany, Joe, I don't know what I will do."

Pretty Kevin is holding his side, which is bleeding as well. "Joe, something don't smell right about your girl, dude. Why she running, man? We all shot up behind that bitch and she runs. What's up?"

"Fellas, I honestly don't know, but I'm going to find out. Y'all get some medical attention. Kevin, call Vernon and let him know what's up. I'm headed to the Hyatt Regency. That's the only place Agent Chase could be headed."

"Joe, you going in alone, that shit ain't smart man, you don't know what you headed into," Little Tiny complains.

"Look, you guys are in no shape to help me right now, and time is of the essence. If Chase has turned bad, she'll be trying to get out of town as quick as possible. There's a lot of money these dudes had access to. I'm quite sure Chase knows all about where that money is. If she has Agent Duvall, I need to get there soon. Dread was working for somebody and Agent Duvall is in grave danger."

"Fuck that Joe, I'm going man," Mo-Mo insists.

I put my hand on his shoulder. "I'll bring her back. You'll bleed to death if you don't get that looked at. You'll only slow me down, Mo-Mo. I'm out of here. Little Tiny, let Commissioner Wayne know what's going on when he arrives."

I run through the crowd, jump on my Harley, and race through the crowded downtown area of Crown Center. I make a call to a lady friend in Jefferson City about my hunch regarding who is behind Dread's black ring of dirty cops.

I park my bike in the circle drive of the vast hotel. At the front desk I show my badge and ask for a pass key for Dread Cattanno's Suite. The hotel manager does as told and asks if I need house security. I explain to him to call and get any guests on that floor off immediately. I explain what's going on, then take the elevator to the Presidential Suite.

I find the door partially ajar and walk in. When I get through the foyer, I find Agent Duvall tied and gagged sitting on the couch with Agent Cheryl Chase sitting in a chair, her thick legs crossed casually with her gun pointed at me as she puts papers into her blue travel bag.

"Going somewhere, Chase?" I ask as I aim my gun at her.

She looks at me and smiles, putting her gun away. "Yes, I am. When I got here Dread's accomplice made me a deal I could not refuse. You could come with me, Joe. You know I have always loved you. We can travel to different countries and see the world!" She stands and hold the blue bag close to her. Her eyes sparkle and her smile is wide and inviting.

"Chase, what do I do about my family that I love? Just forget about them, my job, my friends, and family? You want me to throw all that away? I can't do that. I love Sierra. She's the woman I need, and she's my soul mate. I like you a lot, Chase. You've been through so much, don't throw your career away like this. Too many people have died over this case," I try and reason.

"Joe, you have everything; family, and friends. I don't have that. I've given so much of myself to the Bureau that I can't get back. It's time to think of me now. Dread has over fifty million dollars in untraceable money in different foreign accounts. I have all the account numbers and dummy names he has them under. All that can be ours, Joe," she pleads.

"Not interested. I'm not going anywhere with you, Chase. I'm surprised you'd ask. You know where I stand. I'm here to help you, but not like that. Why do you have Agent Duvall tied up?"

"I'm saving her life, Joe. I'm sorry you're not coming with me. I'm going to miss you," she says as she zips her bag.

I let my gun down for a split second and look at her confused. He comes out of the bedroom, and shoots me in the shoulder. He gets my gun from me and tosses it in the corner.

"Yes, you fucking idiot, you should have listened to her and left when you had the chance!" he yells as spittle flies form his mouth.

"No! You said you wouldn't hurt him, you promised!" Chase yells. She pulls her gun on Missouri Governor Tom Brush and checks my shoulder.

The Governor has held a grudge against Pretty Kevin for pimping Cortney Roberts, his step-daughter. Kevin never realized that the woman was kin to Governor Brush, until after she was kidnapped, raped, and killed by the Missouri River Serial Killer. We also learned the dirty family secret that Governor Brush had impregnated his step-daughter. Pretty Kevin now raises Timmy, now four years old, as his own.

"Well, I lied." He snaps as he steps closer to me. Govenor Brush is a medium built man, with blond hair, small eyes and a square chin. He pale skin is flushed with red. "You and that pimp friend of yours are a big pain in the ass, Detective. I know you called my wife in Jefferson City. I have a loyal staff that's paid for their loyalty. She thinks she's going to divorce me, and I've worked hard to put this black ring together. I've made too many sacrifices and a shit load of cash for either of you to come in and ruin it for me by exposing me to the good people of the state of Missouri. But I promise you, when I finish with you I'm killing her ass, and your pimp friend, Pretty Kevin, too."

Chase cocks her gun and steps closer to him. "So, you think I'm just going to let you get away with this, right?"

"Detective, you're not in a position to do anything about it now, are you?" Two of the Governor's men come in from the bed room with their guns aimed at Chase. "Agent Chase, if you're leaving, you better leave, now. My jet is waiting at the Downtown Municipal Airport to fly you out of the country. Call me as we discussed, once you're in the air. You got forty-five minutes to make it there, so you best be on your way. Make no mistake bitch, if you double cross me with my money, I'll personally hunt you down like a dog, and kill you slow," he threatens, pointing his finger at her.

I lay on the floor bleeding from the shoulder and Agent Duvall sits on the couch, her head is down and hope escapes her eyes.

"Boys, get her out of here!" The Governor screams.

Agent Chase jerks from the men's grasp, knells down, and kisses me on the cheek. She whispers in my ear, "Joe, I love you and I'll make this up to you, I promise. I'll send help. If you ever change your mind about me, I'm yours. Bye, my darling."

She never looks back. She walks out with the accounts and money from Dread's dirty transactions, and leaves us to die. I guess it <u>was</u> all about the money. Money changed people, and God knew what all Dread put her through, but I would have never thought she would have turned on me.

I try and buy some time in hopes that she will at least alert someone of my and Agent Duvall's demise.

"So, Governor Asshole, how much money did you make in this little scheme of yours?"

Governor Brush rushes over to me and strikes me in the face. "You respect my authority, Johnson," he orders as I burst out laughing. "What's so funny, Detective?"

I look him in the eyes, smiling. "You hit like a bitch," I say, laughing again.

He stands over me. "Well, if you think I hit like a bitch, let's see if I shoot like a bitch," he snarls as he shoots me in the thigh.

I grimace. "So, you still haven't answered my question." I tear off part of my shirt and wrap it around my thigh, which bleeds profusely.

Governor Brush walks over and sits across from Agent Duvall, who jumps. The Governor laughs as he rubs and pats her thigh. He turns to face me. "Well, to answer your question, Detective, let's just say, if I let Agent Chase leave with fifty million, my take has been measurably more. Like, one hundred million, more. I don't have a problem telling you this, because when Agent Chase calls me safely in the air from my jet, you will be history, my friend, and your lovely chocolate friend, too. I hope you didn't get too attached to Agent Chase, because after she deposits my money into my account she will be killed as well. I don't like loose ends." He says as he rubs Agent Duvall's ample breasts, winks at her, then checks his watch.

I pull myself up against the chair, and try to get comfortable when I can try to defend myself and Agent Duvall, who is seated directly across from me on the couch. Governor Brush keeps his gaze on me and tilts his curly blond head to warn me not to try anything stupid.

"How did you recruit your men, Governor?"

"It was very simple. Being the Governor, I knew how much the state received from the seizure of drugs and property from law enforcement each year. It's in the billions. I knew that if I could get the right law men behind me, and pay them handsomely, we could funnel millions of tax-free untraceable money, and who would be the wiser."

"But you had to have an inside man, right?"

He shrugged arrogantly. "I just needed an enforcer who could front for me. That's where Dread came in. He had been investigated twice by Internal Affairs for shady dealings and beat both cases. I knew he wasn't stupid and would go for the money. The other men had gambling debts, sick children, materialistic wives, and girlfriends. After a bust we'd tempt them with ten thousand dollars. If they took the bait, they were part of the club. It was very easy and grew faster than we thought. We are in five states and four more were about to come on, until you stuck your nose in it."

"So what did FBI Agent James have to do with it?"

"I had to make sure I knew if you guys were on to us or not. That's why I made sure he had the finances to pay for the investigation. Agent Chase was getting too close. By me paying the finances, I was kept abreast of what was going on. I had the best of both worlds. Dread was falling for Chase and beginning to do stupid things. The fool would have given her my name sooner or later. Agent James had no clue I was the head of the black ring. It was his job to keep me abreast of the investigation. You know how much of a by-the-book fucking guy he is. That's exactly what I needed from that prune."

The Governor's cell phone rings.

"Well Detective, I guess our conversation comes to an end," he winks as he answers, then places the cell on speaker phone.

An engine hums in the background. Chase says, "Governor Brush, I'm on the plane, but it's not your plane. I was able to persuade another pilot to get me out of the country for twenty thousand dollars. Your pilot is still waiting for me at Municipal and your two goons are dead in your limousine in the parking lot at the airport, they should have checked me for weapons. I took the liberty of taking your bank accounts out of your duffle bags in the bedroom, so your one hundred million is mine, too. So, I suggest you get out of there as soon as possible with your stupid ass," she says, laughing into the phone.

The Governor's eyes bulge with rage as his mouth falls open and his hands shake. His thin lips tremble with anger and he turns redder than a tomato on a hot August day.

"You bitch!" He runs and grabs his bag, checking its contents. "You fucking bitch!" Those seem to be the only words he can muster out. He rubs his chin and tries to gather himself, looking around as if trying to find what to say next. "Chase we can work something out. Let's renegotiate."

"That's <u>Ms</u>. Bitch to you. Why do you think I need you? So you can try and kill me later, fool. You been played, like you thought you were playing everybody else. I'll send you a postcard now and then to let you know how I'm spending your money. That's the least I can do. Oh, and I forgot to tell you, I called in a shooting at the hotel and gave them the suite number. I'm sure the Police and FBI are on their way. Thanks again, Governor!" She says, laughing as she hangs up.

The Governor screams. I lunge at him, knocking him backward. I leap into the couch where Agent Duvall sits, knocking it backward to give us a shield from the imminent gun fire. Two shots pierce the couch. Cotton and fabric float in the air in front of us. We duck as low as we can behind the coach.

"Put down the gun or you're dead," a husky, yet familiar voice orders.

"What do I have to lose? Take your best shot!" The Governor screams as four more shots ring out. There is silence and a loud thud.

"Damn dude, you really shot the shit out of him." I exclaim as his aim turns on me.

Brutus and I look at each other. I smile and pull myself over the top of the couch. "Whoa! I'm the good guy! Put that gun down," I order.

"Joe, I'm glad you're okay. I work with Internal Affairs with the Nebraska Police Department. We've been on to Dread for about 24 months now. You and your guys almost blew the case for us. Where's Chase?" He asks as he puts his gun away and unties Agent Duvall.

"She took the money and ran. She on a plane headed somewhere. She was under cover with the FBI," I answer.

"I figured she was a Fed. I can't believe she would turn, but with all she went through, I can understand." Brutus says as he scratches his huge head.

I stumble over to kick the gun away from Governor Brush and check his neck for a pulse. None. Brutus helps me over to the chair I was once leaning against.

"Is he dead, Joe?" Agent Duvall asks as she rubs her bruised wrists.

"Yes, he is," I say with a heavy sigh.

"Brutus, I'm sure glad you are on our team. Joe and I were sure in a bad situation. If I ever get my hands on that heffa, Chase? She just left us for dead, Joe," Agent Duvall says with her hands on her hips.

"Brutus, please hand me my gun in that corner." I place the gun in my holster. "I don't know if we'll ever catch Agent Chase. She's long gone now. By the time we try and find what aircraft and pilot or what flight plan they took, they'll be across the border in either direction."

Agent Duvall brings me some towels out of the bathroom, presses them against the wound on my shoulder, and wraps a couple around my thigh.

Commissioner Wayne, FBI Agent James, and other federal agents and police officers flood the room. We explain what has just transpired and I'm escorted by the paramedics to an awaiting ambulance. My wife and diamond rush to me. My wife looks at me with relief that I'm still alive.

"Baby, you've been hurt. Are you all right?" She asks as she cups my face and kisses me.

Diamond puts her hand on my shoulder as I grimace from the paramedic applying bandages to my leg wound. "I'll be fine. I was shot, but we solved the case. The Governor was behind all this."

Sierra shakes her head in disgust, "What is this world coming to?"

Diamond lets the paramedic get by as he checks my heart rates, pats me on the shoulder and gives me the thumbs up. When he's done she grabs her sister by the hand and pulls her closer to me, "Joe, you need to talk to Sierra. We saw that reporter Tracy on the news. When Sierra heard her call you 'Killer Joe' like she was trying to blow your cover or something, she took me by the hand, pulled me out of your mother's house, and made me get in the car. We drove down to the Plaza and she beat the shit outta that woman with the lady's microphone. I've never seen her like this before. Joe, you're having a bad influence on my sister, man."

Sierra pulls her hand away from Diamond and puts her hands on her hips, "Tracy's been having that coming for years. She could have blown Joe's cover and she had no business calling my man a killer on television, anyway."

Agent Duvall has walked up and says, "I heard that, girl, take up for your man. I would have slapped the heffa for you myself."

I look at all of them. "Y'all some bad ladies." I turn to my wife with love and appreciation. "I'm sorry I put you through this."

"Joe, you know I would die for you, baby," she says as she kisses me. "Let's get you to a hospital."

I smile at my wife and hug her tight, "You tough, baby and cute too. I like that little bad-ass thang you got going on. You go girl!" I tease.

Sierra smiles and raises her eye brow, "Just don't make me go there on you, Mr. Man." We both laugh.

epilogue

A WEEK HAS PASSED SINCE WE ENDED THE BLACK RING CASE. The FBI has found no trace of Chase or the assumed money and bank accounts that had been seized from the drug dealers. Chase got away clean with over one hundred and fifty million dollars in untraceable funds. She sent a letter of resignation to Agent James of the FBI. The letter was postmarked from Belize with no return address.

I received a cashier's check from Chase two days ago postmarked from Jamaica for twenty-five million dollars. I talked to Agent James and Commissioner Wayne and they told me they can't trace the money to any-one, so consider it a gift. Sierra and I have talked about what to do with the money. After we put some aside for the kid's future, we'll share it with our family and friend's. I plan to send money to St. Louis Slim's family as well. I know one thing though; it sure made my two gunshot wounds feel better.

We buried Sweet St. Louis Slim in St. Louis, Missouri two days ago. Mo-Mo and Slim's family made sure he went out in style with his canary-yellow suit and a pair of Stacy Adam's two-tones on his feet. Mo-Mo took it hard, but Agent Duval was right there by his side.

I stand here at my father's gravesite and most of the people have left to return to the church for the dinner. People sure love to eat at funerals. My wife, kids, mother, brothers, and sisters, Pretty Kevin, Mo-Mo, Agent Jason "Little Tiny" Phillips, Agent Epiphany Duvall, Agent James, Commissioner Wayne, and my best friend, Detective Vernon Brown, wait by the limousines and their cars for me as I say my final goodbye to my father.

It is a beautiful overcast morning and the birds are chirping and flying around in the gray skies that are kissed by puffy storm clouds. I hold a single rose in my hand and adjust my crutch under my arm to support my bad leg, which is healing from the gunshot wound. The grave diggers look on from a distance.

"Daddy, you meant the world to me. You were a man of few words, you led by example, always had a big smile, and a loving laugh. Thank you for what you did for the family and the sacrifices you made for us. I will always remember you and keep you in my heart. I know you're looking down from heaven and will be watching out for us. I promise to make sure Mom is taken care of. Put in a good word to God for me." I smile and toss the rose into the grave, and wave the grave diggers over to finish their job.

I walk over to my family and closest friends and we depart to the family dinner. I look back as we drive off in the limousine and the rain starts to fall. In the distance, I see Agent Cheryl Chase appear from behind a grave stone. She waves at me. I nod, sit back in my seat, and smile. I don't know what she went through when she was with Dread, but evidently, it was pretty bad. I say a little prayer for her and hope she will be okay as she stands in the graveyard as though she's being baptized in the black rain.

about the author

Vincent Alexandria - "If Walls Could Talk", "Postal Blues", "Black Rain", & "Poetry from the Bottom of My Heart." (We Must X-L Publishing Co.) He is an author, actor, producer, director, composer, lyricist, vocalist, screen writer, and musician. He is the father of four children. He holds a Masters degree in literature at Baker University and holds a Bachelor's degree in Psychology from Rockhurst College. He's a GED Teacher with the EVENSTART Program in Kansas City, MO. His vision for the Brother 2 Brother Symposium is to enlighten men and women in reading and comprehension to enhance their quality of life. Having nationally published authors show a commitment to their communities and give back to their readers in gratitude of what they have done for them and their careers.